BEDROCK

THE BEDROCK SERIES | BOOK ONE

BRITNEY KING

WWW.BRITNEYKING.COM

ALSO BY BRITNEY KING

Breaking Bedrock

Beyond Bedrock

The Social Affair

Water Under The Bridge

Dead In The Water

Come Hell or High Water

Around The Bend

Somewhere With You

Anywhere With You

BEDROCK

BRITNEY KING

COPYRIGHT

Hot Banana Press

Front Cover Design by Lisa Wilson

Back Cover Design by Britney King

Cover Image by Sebastian Kullas

Copy Editing by TW Manuscript Services

Proofread by Proofreading by the Page

First Edition: 2013

ISBN: 978-0-9892184-0-5 (Paperback)

ISBN: 978-9892184-1-2 (All E-Books)

britneyking.com

To Nannie
with love.

CHAPTER ONE

Sometimes you have to look back in order to move forward. Sometimes you find yourself in a situation where that is the *only* thing you can do, which is exactly the situation Addison Greyer found herself in when she awoke in a hazy fog with something warm and wet trickling down her face. She tried to shift, to pull herself up, but it was useless. Her body hurt and nothing was right. *This is what dying feels like.* She did her best to recall what happened *before* she was in this predicament, but nothing came and it took so much effort to try and remember. It was almost more than she could manage. She told herself to breathe. But even that hurt. She brought her fingers to her face, or at least she imagined she did. It was hard to tell. She couldn't see, she couldn't feel, not really. It was cold, *so cold.* Addison inhaled carefully. *Where am I?*

Before her brain could grasp the answer, she felt herself slipping backward, back into the darkness, back to sleep. She willed herself to wake up, to open her eyes, but it was of no use. Her brain and her eyes refused to cooperate with one another. She couldn't focus on a single thought and she went in and out of consciousness several times before finally waking to the clanking of chains. Metal on metal. One second she was here and another *there*. *What were those crazy boys doing now? And why can't I wake up and make them stop?*

Her head throbbed. Her heart raced and she curled further into a ball. It hurt to move, not that she could move much and there was that sound again. *Wake up, damn it. Wake up.* Finally, her eyes fluttered open, though just barely. She could see a blurry figure standing a few feet in front of her but her eyes still refused to focus and she was too dizzy in any case to determine who it was. *Focus, she told herself. What do you see, taste, smell, touch? Use your senses.* The metallic scent of blood overwhelmed her. Aside from a dry mouth, that's all she could taste. *Blood. Is this a dream and if so, how do I wake up?* She felt the chill of the concrete beneath her. Her head was too heavy to lift, but she forced herself to do it anyway. She wiggled her toes. *She wasn't dead.* Again, she heard the clanking of the chains, which made her breath catch and then a male voice. "Wake up," the voice demanded.

Who was he? Did she know that voice? She thought before she felt herself start slipping again. Suddenly she was jolted awake by something slashing her skin. That did it. She opened her eyes just as the leather whip slashed again.

"Wake up, it's time to talk," the booming voice commanded. It was muffled, disguised, it sounded as though she were hearing it from under water.

Oh my God. How did I get here?

Addison forced herself to focus. *Pain tends to help people with that.* She surveyed her surroundings and quickly realized she'd woken up in her very own version of hell. Glancing around the room, she realized it resembled a dungeon, the kind you might see on TV. The only lighting was a single bulb hanging in the far corner of the room. The room itself was cold, dark, and damp. *Basement like.* Thinking it was sweat, she reached up and wiped at the wetness on her forehead. But when she pulled her hand back all she saw was red. *Her hand instinctively went to her neck.* There was a chain around her throat, shackles on both her hands and feet and her clothes had been removed. Addison tried to get a look at the man, at the voice who spoke to her, but he was behind her, beyond her range of sight, somewhere in the dark. Plus, everything was so foggy. *Where are the boys?* She gasped. *Where are my kids? Does he have them, too?* She started to sob.

The whip struck her again. She didn't care. She couldn't make the sobs quit coming. Struck, again and again, she did her best to shield her face and withdrew into herself trying to make her body as small as possible. As she crawled into a ball, she felt a tugging on the chain around her neck. She was choking. She couldn't breathe. If it didn't stop soon, the darkness was going to take her once again and she was powerless to stop it.

The deep voice spoke again. "Look— we can do this the easy way or the hard way. It's your choice. I actually prefer the hard way, so keep it up if you like. Just know...next come the shocks."

I'm going to die here. Oh God. No, not like this, please. Please, not like this. She thought of her children. *What would they tell them?* She shook her head hoping it might help. It didn't. *Just do what he says. It's your job to figure out what he wants.*

It took everything she had to pull herself up to a sitting position but she held her palms out and then she did it. Eventually, she managed to prop herself up against the far wall of the cage. This is when he came into view, at least partially. He was wearing a ski mask with dark glasses over the eyeholes and that's when Addison realized, *he could be anybody.* Still, she knew she needed to put as much distance as she could between them. Addison felt her survival instincts kicking in.

She met his gaze head on. Not that she could see him, not really. But he could see her. He sat in a chair opposite the cage and watched her. Addison didn't speak. She wanted to beg, to plead for her life. She wanted her kids and her clothes, she wanted out of there. Something deep down told her to keep her mouth shut. So instead of saying all the things she wanted to say she simply watched him, refusing to take her eyes away, her mind running a thousand miles a minute. The two of them stayed that way for an eternity, chills ran through her, tears fell involuntarily, but she didn't look away. Until, finally, he got up from the chair and ascended stairs that were just beyond her line of sight.

He was gone. She took a deep breath in and held it before exhaling slowly. *He's gone now. He can't hurt you. Breathe. But he's coming back. Breathe.* Addison felt herself slipping again, back into the fog, and she didn't fight it. She laid herself down on the concrete floor, slowly and so carefully, unable to take the pain of each small movement. She was so tired, so weak, but it was the blood, and the awareness that he would be back that scared her most. He wanted her to suffer; that much was clear. The fog seemed like the only respite she had. It beckoned her. And she welcomed it.

ADDISON DREAMT she was sitting on the porch swing watching the boys play with Max. They would run the entire length of the yard, and he would chase after them. They were laughing, she was laughing, and it was nice to feel the warm sunshine on her face. She was glad she could feel the breeze blow across her skin. But then the opera music began and nothing seemed right. *Why in the world would the sounds of the opera fill her backyard?* Suddenly, Addison felt her arms and her legs being pulled in opposite directions. Hard. She opened her eyes and she wasn't in her backyard at all, she was back in that cage, back in the dungeon and she was being stretched out from opposite ends. It hurt— although, for some reason the pain was dull—below the surface as though she were barely feeling it. She felt the sting of the whip across her belly, followed shortly by warm blood dripping from where the leather met her skin. She felt that. It wasn't dull. It was sharp and jarring. *But why? She asked herself. Why is he doing this? Why me?*

"Didn't I tell you to wake up?" the man said. His voice wasn't clear, she realized he was trying to disguise it, and this concerned her more than anything. If he'd planned to kill her right away, he wouldn't care whether or not she saw his face or heard him speak. But he did.

"You disobeyed me. I've told you and I've told you and I've told you. It's time to talk. But no. You're lazy. Just like the rest of them. I just hope you're a little smarter." He cocked his head. "Well… are you?" he shouted. "Are you ever going to learn your lesson?"

He walked around her until she could feel his body heat. He placed a blindfold over her eyes. She struggled but it was pointless.

"You aren't allowed to sleep," he said.

"If I find you sleeping again, the punishment is going to be worse than a whipping. Do you understand?"

Addison said nothing. She saw the hand that contained the whip rise. She held her breath just before it struck her across her thighs. It wasn't so much the pain but rather the sound of the leather hitting her skin that made her sick, it made her stomach want to empty its contents.

"So, are we clear Mrs. Greyer?" he asked toying with the whip. "From now on, when I speak to you, you show some respect."

Addison nodded. He addressed her by name, which

11

meant he knew who she was. It also meant this was not random; it was not some sort of mistake.

"That a girl. I always took you for a quick learner."

She thought about her surroundings once again. If she was gagged, that had to mean he was afraid people would hear her. *Didn't it?* She recalled four corners of the room. Even before he'd blindfolded her, it was too dark to make out much, but she could feel that the walls were made of stone. And then, there was that smell. The stench alone over-whelmed her senses. It was pungent, a mixture of urine and alcohol standing out most. *Where am I? His basement? A warehouse?*

She felt herself floating upward. She thought she was passing out again, or perhaps this was really it. Her eyes grew wide and she struggled against her restraints.

"It's the drugs that make you feel like that," he said. "Well, that and fear…"

Suspended in the air, naked, bleeding, and weak, all she could think about was closing her eyes and pretending to be in her backyard with her children, the sun on her face. So, that's what she did. She needed to remain positive, to think of anything that would help her escape this hell. Addison forced herself to count. She was afraid she was going to lose consciousness and she'd heard his warning about sleep. He wanted her awake and now she understood why. She listened as he toyed with his whips and spikes, his tools of the trade. That was the thing about losing your senses. Everything else became more acute. This was a form of intimidation, she knew. *But how? How did she know this?*

"I know you're probably thirsty. Hungry. But since you haven't yet learned to follow the rules, you get nothing."

After a bit of tinkering, she heard him turn and once again walked up the dark stairs without a word. It may have been hours or mere minutes. She couldn't be sure. There was no concept of time. She had no idea what day of the week it was, how long she'd been there, or whether it was even day or night. It was with this thought that the tears came again. Only Addison didn't sob this time. She was too weak. Instead, silent tears ran down her cheeks, falling onto her bare breasts. She tried her best to fight off sleep and when she caught herself dozing off, she'd play games with herself, recalling a memory of her boys, and then she'd replay it over and over in her mind in order to keep herself awake. She knew she had to get through this and to do that she'd have to stay alert, if she wanted to get out alive. But then, she had to get out alive. There was no other option. Her family needed her. Her children needed her.

Throughout the time that the man was away, Addison dozed off and on despite her best attempts. But it was fitful sleep at best. When she allowed herself to close her eyes, she made sure her sleep was light, not so different from the early days, when her boys were first born and she'd force herself to stay awake to check on them, to make sure they were still breathing.

Eventually, she heard the door creak and her eyes snapped open. Her heart raced as she listened to his footsteps fall on the stairs. Her stomach churned, unsure of what to expect. When he saw that she was awake, he chuckled. As he walked towards her, Addison's pulse raced. The closer he got, the more she squirmed. She didn't want to have this reaction, but it was innate. Her brain screamed for her to be still and to remain calm and yet the rest of her body betrayed her, giving away her fear.

She felt him remove the gag. She trembled at his proximity. "There, there. Easy does it," he whispered, trailing his cold hand down her cheek. "Don't bother screaming. No one will hear you."

Addison tensed as he moved his hand away. When she felt

it on her skin again, he was holding a straw to her lips. "If we don't get some water in you, I'll have gone to all this trouble for nothing," he warned. "Now, be a good girl and take a drink."

She did as he said, taking a small sip at first, but then she couldn't stop. She kept drinking until she choked, and he pulled the straw away. "Ok, I think that's enough," he said pulling the glass away and then replacing her gag. She held her breath as he took a step back and walked around the back of her. It made her uneasy when she couldn't get a sense of where he was or what he was doing—but then, she was just as uneasy as when she could. "You look so beautiful," he murmured. "In fact, I don't think I've seen anything more beautiful in my life."

After several moments, he walked back around and stopped just in front of her. He removed the blindfold and then he stood there for a moment as her eyes adjusted, considering her. He tinkered with her chains, and when he seemed satisfied with how she was displayed, he stepped back and closed the door to the cage. She watched as he sat in a metal folding chair just outside the cage. He unbuckled his belt and removed it, laying it at his feet. Her pulse quickened and she couldn't help but look away. "Look at me, damn it," he ordered and she did as she was told. Hot, wet tears fell onto her cheeks as she met his gaze. His eyes tracked south as did hers and she could see that he was erect. "It's my turn to give you a show," he said as he began stroking himself. It took everything she had not to look away. Swallowing hard against the gag, she felt bile rise in her throat and she wondered what would happen if she were to be sick. *He will kill you.* She held her breath. She couldn't help herself. It seemed to go on forever, and she grew dizzy as the man stared a hole through her.

When he was finished, he stood, picked up his belt and

unlocked the door to the cage. The hairs on the back of her neck stood as he walked around her, just as he had the time before. He circled slowly a few times and then finally paused behind her, once again out of eyesight. He replaced the blindfold and then the gag. When he'd finished, she heard him raise the belt as she braced herself for the blow she knew was coming. The belt struck across her rear, forcing all the air from her lungs. Addison gasped; she moaned and tried to say her pleas against the gag. He struck her once, twice, three times until she lost count, each blow worse than the last. Eventually, unable to take any more, long after her silent pleas ran out, as did her cries, she hung her head.

"You're a bad girl, watching me like that. You should be ashamed," he told her as he exited the cage. She listened as he placed the lock on the door. Her head felt too heavy to lift and she'd already come to her decision: if he killed her, he killed her. She could hear him dressing. She could hear his footsteps as he walked towards the dark corner. She flinched when she heard the cranking sound. It almost forced her to look up. *Almost.* Her body stiffened which only worsened the pain. She was being lowered and every inch felt like a mile. Slowly, she descended towards the cold concrete beneath her. When her body hit bottom, she'd expected it to hurt. Instead, she sighed at how good it felt against her wounded backside. She wept long after she heard the man turn and walk up the stairs. *He could be anyone, she thought. But he knew her, and he wanted her to suffer.*

As Addison lay there on the cold, hard floor, wounded and bleeding, she began to think back, trying to recall how she could have possibly ended up here. She began drifting, unaware of whether she was dreaming or awake. The images were crystal clear as they came. Piece by piece the inner-workings of her life appeared vividly before her eyes. Everything was there, every bit of it and was so colorful, so vibrant, that she wondered if she was dying. *Isn't that what everyone said happened before you die?* Still, she watched, mesmerized, all the while praying the answers she needed would come— something—*anything* that would set her free and not death, as she feared.

CHAPTER TWO

A ddison was six the first time she thought about the man she would marry. Immediately, she was transported back to the room in her grandparents home where she spent hours, so many hours, in front of that TV. It was there it all started, in a sense, it was there she first imagined what he'd look like, how they would meet, how she would finally, once and for all, get her happily ever after. She had seen enough fairytales on TV to know exactly what it would be like. It was rough being an only child. It was even worse that she lived with old people. That's what the kids at school said anyway. No matter what they said, she had TV and her fairytales and she could always depend on them to keep her entertained. Growing up in a retirement community her options weren't exactly wide open. At least she had a roof over her head, her grandmother often reminded her. It's too bad a roof doesn't make people happy, she said once and only once. After that she learned what it meant to eat your words.

Addison could imagine that their home was once a happy place, but she'd never known it to be so. It was quiet and stuffy. Her grandparents' rarely spoke to her, and while they cared enough to keep her alive, that was pretty much the extent of it. To them, Addison was invisible. That's not to say she really tried all that hard to get their attention. Mostly, she tried to stay out of the way, under the radar. Her grandparents were sad enough as it was, she surely didn't want to make things any worse for them, so the older she got, the smaller she tried to become. She learned early on to keep her head down, and the longer she did, the less everyone suffered.

Her mother should have been better about keeping her head down, that's what her grandfather liked to say. Even though he never really expanded upon his sentiment beyond that, Addison always assumed he was talking about her. Her parents were seventeen when her mother got pregnant. While she didn't know the full story, she had gotten bits and pieces of it over the years, most of them coming from her great-aunt Sara, who loved to tell Addison stories of her mother, Constance. She, too, was an only child, the apple of her parents' eye. She was smart, kind, and beautiful, the kind of child that parents dream of having, that's what Sara said, anyway. Although, Addison always wondered whether it was really true or just one of those things you said about a person after they were dead. Constance was on the fast track to Princeton when she met Addison's father at a soccer game in her last year of high school. Her parents insisted he wasn't right for her, he wasn't good enough, he was going nowhere fast. He would steal her dreams, they warned. Against her grandparents' wishes, Addison's parents had secretly been dating for a few months when her mother found out she was pregnant. Coming from a strict Catholic family, her mother knew abortion was not an option. And when Constance finally got the nerve to tell her parents, they insisted that she give the baby up for adoption.

Addison's father, Michael, begged her mother not to give

her up. He proposed marriage and tried his best to prove that they could build a life together. With time quickly running out, just two months before her due date, Constance finally agreed to marry him. Together they concocted a plan to forge the parental consent form required to get married and cross state lines, where they would get hitched and hide out until her due date. Constance was sure once they saw the baby, they'd fall in love and agree to help out. And, if not, well, they'd have each other. But that was where everything went terribly wrong. Two hundred miles from home, a drunk driver veered into their lane, forcing them off the highway and into a tree. Badly injured, her mother made it to the hospital where doctors delivered Addison who weighed exactly three pounds and, aside from being tiny and premature, was mostly okay. Her mother on the other hand succumbed to her injuries shortly after she was delivered.

As luck would have it, Addison was a dead ringer for her mother, which in addition to grief she guessed, was why her grandparents decided to keep her. Her grandmother had even told her as much once, that they had lost the one and only thing they loved, and since she was the only piece they had left of Constance, they couldn't bear to let her go, too. She had always sensed that it was the guilt that drove the decision to keep her. Her upbringing certainly proved that it wasn't one made out of love or concern.

Her father, Michael, had wanted to keep and raise her. But her grandparents hired a team of attorneys who quickly solidified in his mind what he already knew, that there was no way that an eighteen-year-old boy with nothing could win the case, unless you count good intentions, which as it turns out, don't hold up in court. Her grandparents told her through the years that they hoped her father had learned his lesson. He had taken their daughter from them, and the least they could do was return the favor. Although her grandparents spent a small fortune trying to prevent it, a fact of which they boasted proudly, Michael was granted visitation. Addison remembered fondly the time she spent with him until she was around six or so and he moved to Colorado, where he started a new family. He had a new life, a fresh start, he called it, one without so much sadness, she assumed, because after he moved, the phone calls and letters grew further and further apart each year, until she rarely heard from him at all.

IT WAS AN UNASSUMING, chilly, overcast fall morning the day Addison met the man who would later change her life, become her husband and father her three children. While it was just another ordinary day, in retrospect, the moment Addie met Patrick, though she would never admit it to anyone other than herself, she *knew* he was the one. It would take him a little more time. But Addison had decided, she wanted *him* and would settle for nothing less.

She had broken up with her boyfriend of three years the summer before, because, while he was the perfect boyfriend for her grandparents, she knew, she had always known, that he was not the one. It's not that she wanted to hurt him but Addison had plans and he wasn't in them. Her friends continuously gave her flack for having her whole life mapped out. And she did. She knew she would graduate, get married, and have two kids and the white picket fence, perhaps even a dog. She made it clear that her home would be a happy one, with dinner parties and lots of friends, and her boyfriend, the one her grandparents were in love with, he didn't like parties. She wanted someone who wanted what she wanted and she intended to have just that.

In the meantime, though, she intended to enjoy college.

She wasn't looking for a boyfriend, much less a husband; she was looking to have the time of her life. She was looking for people, she was looking for company. In fact, she said it was the first time in as long as she could remember that she didn't feel lonely. A prisoner who had escaped her captors she laughed, one night after a few too many, and admitted she finally felt free. Always the life of the party, Addison reinvented herself her freshman year, after all, no one knew her at Baines. Seeing that she could be anyone, anything she wanted to be, she chose to be audacious. And, while everyone else her age seemed not to take life too seriously, she was known amongst her circle of friends as a popular over-achiever with a list of goals a mile long, of which she was promptly ticking things off. People looked up to her and she knew it.

Somewhere down the line, on her list of things to achieve was to find a good man, one who checked all the boxes. It turned out this didn't exactly happen in the way she envisioned it, but it made for a great story, nonetheless.

"THIS IS GOING to make a great story," the deep voice said, jarring Addison awake. She blinked once, then twice, before opening her eyes completely. "You have no idea how long I've waited for this," he added, as he arranged her arms the way he seemed to want them to be. Addison watched as he paused and stepped back. Next, he adjusted her restraints, before removing them altogether. He grabbed her hair, "Up you go," he said, lifting her by her forearms. She tried to stand but her legs buckled underneath her. The man grabbed her hair. "Do you want to make this hard?"

Addison shook her head; her eyes grew wide as she watched him pull a syringe from his pocket. She moaned against her gag, pleading with him incoherently. She'd do anything to avoid whatever drug it was he was injecting her with.

He cocked his head. "Oh, you have something to say…" he asked as he studied her naked body. He was wearing a different ski mask than the one he'd worn before, but the glasses were the same. He stared at her for a long while taking the back of his hand and running it up the length of her and back down again. Her breath quickened and tears spilled over onto her cheeks. Eventually, he removed the gag. "I'd like to hear you beg, in your own voice."

Addison swallowed the lump in her throat. Her mouth was so dry that it took several tries before she was able to form words. "I'll do whatever you want," she pleaded. "Just, please, no more of that."

The man placed his hands on his hips. "You don't like needles?"

She shook her head profusely. "I don't like the way it makes me feel…"

"Too bad," he said, grabbing her by the hair. He pulled her in the direction he wanted her to go. "You're not the one in charge here, are you? This isn't your story. It's mine."

"Please," Addison cried. "I'll do—"

"You'll do whatever I tell you to do," he said, releasing her hair and shoving her to the floor. She landed with a thud that knocked the wind out of her.

Addison watched as he pulled a lever lifting a square piece from the floor. "Crawl in," he ordered. She shook her head. "I said, CRAWL IN."

She didn't budge but she couldn't make the sobs stop coming either. "Damn it," he spat. "In or I inject you with this," he told her, holding up the syringe. She watched as he removed the cap using his teeth.

"Please, don't… I just want to go home…I have—"

"You have ten seconds is what you have. NOW. GET. IN. Believe me, when you're out of it, it makes it a lot harder to keep the critters off."

Addison sobbed. He took her by the hair and drug her to the trap door. She eyed the syringe and then crawled in. "Why are you doing this?" she asked.

He laughed. "Because I can," he told her, after considering her for a moment. "That's something you'd do well to learn. Lots of people simply do things because they can."

"I—"

"Oh," he called, cutting her off. "I almost forgot. I hope you don't mind critters."

Addison cried knowing what was to come. She didn't want to be buried alive. She hated confined spaces. "Isn't it funny?" he chuckled, as he lowered the small door. "We're all just worm food in the end."

She laid there in the dark, counting, just to keep herself from losing it altogether. He—or someone—had dug a hole in the ground, no more than a crawl space. With just enough room to turn from side to side, there wasn't much to work with. Every once and awhile, Addison would feel something crawling on her. She'd find the insect, brush it off. Before long, she began to bury them in the dirt; thinking that if she could just dig far enough, then maybe she'd wind up in the center of the earth. Maybe she could dig her way out. At some point, he lifted the door and stabbed the needle in her arm. Before long, all there was was darkness.

It was a crisp fall Texas morning that would shape a good portion of her life. But it was clumsiness that would set into motion a chain of events that would take her down a long and winding path she hadn't seen coming. Addison was walking from the library to the cafeteria, either lost in thought or thinking about what was on the lunch menu when her phone rang, startling her. Flinging her book bag off her shoulder, she dug blindly in search of the phone, she felt her fingertips graze it, but then she lost her footing, slipped, and nearly toppled over. In an attempt to avoid landing flat on her face, she dropped the books in her hands and let her bag fall to the ground. Thankfully she was able to catch herself from hitting the pavement. As she bent down to retrieve her things scattered among the lawn, she bumped into something, or rather, someone. Dazed and a little shaken, looking up she blinked rapidly, considering her eyes might be deceiving her. There, before her, was perhaps the most beautiful man she had ever seen. Studying his face, she thought for a second that he looked familiar, but she couldn't place him.

"I'm sorry. Do I know you?" she asked, feeling herself blush.

He shook his head and then extended his hand. "Don't think so," he said. "I'm Patrick," he smiled. "Patrick Greyer."

She didn't respond, not right away, all she could do was stare. The first thing she realized about Patrick Greyer was that he was kind. After he gathered her things, he insisted on walking her to the cafeteria just to make sure she was all right. Making small talk, he explained that he was from Dallas and was majoring in finance. Addison didn't speak much, only enough to answer his questions. She was majoring in communications and hoped to go to work in marketing when she graduated. Patrick told her he knew what he was doing after graduation; he was on the fast track to gain employment at Morgan, Lehman & Scott, where he was already interning. He was sure of himself and she liked that. So, when the time for their next class came, Patrick casually mentioned having dinner the following Friday, how could she have said anything other than yes? The two of them exchanged phone numbers, and that was that.

Only it wasn't because she waited for a call that didn't appear to be coming. The waiting game was excruciating for Addison. Every time the phone rang, she made a beeline for it. She held her breath and crossed her fingers. And every time it wasn't Patrick, her stomach sank and then she'd pout relentlessly. Three days went by and no phone call came. *Had she been mistaken? Had she just imagined that there was an attraction? Was he just being polite asking her to dinner? No. At least she didn't think so. Maybe he lost her number.* Finally, just about the time she put it out of her mind, the call came. That day, when the phone rang, she knew it was him.

"Hello," she answered, a little too enthusiastically.

"Hi, Addison?"

"Yes."

"Um…This is Patrick. We met in the commons the other day…"

She smiled into the phone. His voice was even deeper than she remembered. She shut her eyes, lifted up a silent thank you, and smiled. "Uh . . . Yes, I remember."

"Good. So . . . I was wondering if you still wanted to have dinner Friday?"

She silently screamed, doing a little happy dance around the room "Yeah, of course."

"Great. I'll pick you up at seven o'clock then."

She plopped down on her bed and sighed. "Perfect. Oh, and Patrick?"

"Yeah?"

"I'm looking forward to it."

She heard him take a deep breath in and let it out. "Me, too," he said.

THE NEXT FEW days both dragged on and went by in a blur. True to form, Addison started planning her outfit Wednesday evening. Wondering what she should wear, she realized that she hadn't even thought to ask where he was taking her. This was the first, first date that she could remember. She had been with Jason for so long that he was practically part of her family. They never needed to make plans; it was just assumed that he would be there, that whatever it was they were doing, they were doing it together. This is what she missed the most. It wasn't so much Jason per se, but always having someone to do things with.

Dating was all-new to her. She wasn't even sure if she could technically count what she was doing as dating. Most of the time, the boys on campus simply asked to meet up with her and a group of friends. They'd ask what party she'd planned to attend and then there they would be. This time it felt different. Patrick felt different, which was, in part, why there was so much riding on this one date and why she insisted her outfit had to be absolutely perfect.

Addison knew how to dress for her body—always had. Tall and slender like her mother had been, she had curves in all the right places. It made dressing the part fairly simple. Still, she swore she didn't have the fashion sense *nor* the clothing budget that her roommate Jessica had, which was exactly who she went to in order to help her find the perfect first-date outfit. Jessica was, of course, thrilled to help. While Jess wasn't quite as fortunate to have the body type that Addison had, she was an expert at putting things together. More importantly, when Jessica couldn't figure it out for herself, she was lucky that she had an unlimited budget and access to a personal shopper at almost every high-end store in town.

The only granddaughter of an oil tycoon, practically born with a silver spoon in her mouth into a family where they never wanted for anything a day in their lives, Jessica and Addison were opposites in every way, and unlikely friends. At 5'2", Jessica was short with an athletic build. She had long chestnut hair and eyes to match. Jessica was everything that Addie was not: rich, worry-free, and extremely smart especially where people skills came into play. While Addison was organized and by the minute, Jessica was fly by the seat of her pants. While Addie had to study for days, sometimes even weeks to ace an exam, Jessica only had to show up.

Addie had dozens of potential date outfits lined up and strewn about her bed when Jessica came bursting through the door. She took one look at her friend's perplexed expression and exclaimed, "Oh, no, no, no. You cannot wear this on a date! Or this, or this or this…"

"It's all I've got," Addison said looking away.

Jessica could see the disappointment on her friend's face. "Well, then. You're in luck. I decided yesterday that this occasion calls for a special trip to Neiman's. So, I booked us an appointment with my favorite stylist."

"No—" Addison said. "I can't—"

"You can. We have to be there in thirty, so hurry up."

"Jess—"

Jessica held up her hand cutting Addison off. "Oh, and by the way, I checked out this Patrick character, and I'm not so sure. From what I've heard, he's mostly a loner, though a smart one: valedictorian and currently sitting at the top of our class. So, I guess, *maybe* there is potential. But you need someone who is social, not someone who stays holed up in his apartment and rarely dates."

Addison picked up a dress and rolled her eyes. "Uh huh. How do you know all of this, anyway?"

"I asked around," she shrugged. "And I may or may not have had Perry sneak a peek at his student file," Jessica added, with her signature sly grin.

"That's illegal. And Perry needs to stop doing everything you ask of him. If he weren't so in love with you, surely he would know better."

Frowning, Jessica picked up a shirt and threw it at her. "He is not in love with me," she exclaimed rolling her eyes. "But whatever. Let's go."

Jessica, usually right, was also correct about the stylist at Niemen's. Although, Addison knew that she had nowhere near the kind of money required to buy the dress and shoes that were put together for her, she knew better than to argue with Jessica. While she hated it, she knew that Jessica enjoyed buying her things. She saw it as Jessica making her a charity case, but deep down Addison knew there was more to it than that. "I have the money," Jess shrugged. "So why not use it on something worthwhile?"

"I can't accept this," Addison told her.

Jessica laughed. "I hadn't realized you had the option."

Despite the fact that Addison had tons of homework and a paper due the next day, she agreed.

Later that night, although she was exhausted, she found herself lying there staring at the ceiling, unable to sleep, and wondering how tomorrow's date would go. *Would she say the right things? Would he like her? Would she like him?* And when it came time to discuss her childhood, where would she find the words? *How exactly do you tell someone that you've never in your life ever really felt loved?* She sighed at the thought, but mostly, she wondered just how long could she put off having that conversation.

CHAPTER THREE

Patrick picked Addie up outside her dorm exactly as he had said, promptly at seven o'clock. It was a warm fall night, she recalled that the air smelled of fresh cut grass, these were things she knew she'd never forget. Seeing him standing there waiting, leaning against the stoop waiting on *her*, well, that was almost too much. *Damn.* She took a deep breath and paused, taking him in.

While she stood there mesmerized, wondering whether to run for him or head for the hills, pondering how she could keep from messing this up, Patrick looked up at her and smiled. Her heart sank; the butterflies in the pit of her stomach churned and she was certain she hadn't felt these feelings in a very long time, if ever. *So, this is what love feels like,* she thought throwing up her hands, rushing down the stairs toward the future. Stopping just in front of him and cocked her head. She hadn't planned what she might say.

Thankfully, Patrick bent down and hugged her. "You look nice," he whispered in her ear. She pulled away first. At 6'4", Patrick towered over her. Feeling his breath on her skin made her dizzy but it was the dimples she saw when she looked up at him that nearly did her in. *I hope our children get those dimples.*

"What now?" she said unable to think of anything else.

"I'm taking you to a local restaurant that I've heard good things about... it features fresh, local food," he told her studying her face. *How am I supposed to eat at a time like this,* she thought.

"I hope that's ok," he said, holding the passenger door open as she climbed in.

Unable to believe her luck, she smiled, feeling incredibly grateful for chance meetings. "That's perfect."

AS FAR AS first dates go, theirs was flawless.

It felt different for Addison; this time she actually cared. Patrick seemed genuinely interested in her, asking questions in all the right places. She was sure of herself, he'd said, and he liked that about her.

Still Addison didn't want to get her hopes up, so when she sensed a little hesitation on Patrick's part, she decided to give him an out. "You know, I have to be honest —"

"I like honesty," he said.

She looked up and swallowed. "Good. It's just...well...I'm pretty happy with life as it is and I don't want to mess it up. I'm not really looking to date, and I'm sure as hell not looking for anything serious. Not right now."

Patrick picked up his wine and took a sip, his eyes never leaving hers. "That's the best thing you could've said, actually."

ALTHOUGH NEITHER OF them was willing to label their relationship one way or another, Addison and Patrick found themselves pretty much a couple from that first date on.

They dated smoothly for two years, becoming almost inseparable. For the most part, their relationship was ideal. They were the best of friends, and, as Jessica liked to remind her, their sex life was "to die for." For the first time ever, if Addison were being honest with herself, she felt loved. Patrick adored her, perhaps even more than she adored him.

Then came their senior year. It was the year that would put them to the test. Though it was never really said, Addison knew that Patrick's family didn't approve of her, and she suspected that this was the reason Patrick didn't speak much of the future or specifically, of their future beyond graduation. Patrick had mentioned a few times that his parents had a girl picked out they hoped he'd marry. But that he wasn't thinking about marriage. While she didn't know much, she knew from the beginning that Patrick's childhood was very different from her own. He grew up in an upscale-gated community in Dallas, Texas. His father was a doctor and his mom a housewife, who according to Patrick, mostly played tennis and planned exclusive dinner parties. He had an older sister, Jennifer, although he spoke even less about her than he did his parents. Needless to say, if Addison knew why Patrick's parents disapproved of their relationship, she didn't say.

But also, fair was fair. She didn't want to talk about her family and she never felt like forcing him to talk about his. In fact, she put off telling him about her parents, or lack thereof, for as long as she possibly could, finally only telling him that her mother had died and that her grandparents had raised her. Patrick didn't pry or ask further questions, and for that she was grateful. As time went on, she gave him pieces, brief snippets of her life growing up, but never the whole truth. That was the thing about people like Patrick and Jessica, they were idealists and Addison didn't want to be the person to shatter those ideals.

~

EVENTUALLY, Patrick invited Addison to dinner with his parents when they stopped into town. Still, she hadn't really spent any significant amount of time with them and so when Patrick informed her that his parents had invited them to their lake house for the weekend the summer before their final semester, she was ecstatic insisting that they were finally coming around. But she read otherwise in his demeanor and so she hesitated, making excuses as to why she couldn't go. In the end, however, she gave in, knowing Jess was right when she told her that it was now or never.

The lake house, like the Greyer's, was immaculate and formal. While the Greyer's put on a friendly face in front of their son, Addison was otherwise given the cold shoulder. To add insult to injury, she couldn't help but notice they went out of their way to make sure that whenever they spoke of Patrick's future, she wasn't included, which they did, a lot. It was clear pretty quickly why she'd been invited. They wanted to put her in her place; they wanted to let her know where things stood.

On their second night there, after an uncomfortable interrogation about her childhood and family at the dinner table, courtesy of Jenn, Patrick's older sister, Addison and Patrick had it out. She requested they leave the following morning and accused his family of insinuating that she wasn't good enough for him, which Patrick flat out denied. To make matters worse, Patrick was different around his family. He was quiet and distant when it came to her and yet needy and child-like in the face of his family. This made her question whether she knew him at all.

When he called her crazy, she began throwing her things into her bag. He surveyed the room. "What are you doing?"

"What does it look like I'm doing? I'm leaving."

Patrick sat on the edge of the bed and stared at the floor. "Stay, Addison," he sighed.

She didn't hesitate. She didn't stop packing.

"They'll come around. But, I think you're making a big deal out of nothing..."

Her face grew red and she threw her hands up. "Of course, you do. Don't accuse me of being crazy. I know that your parents think I'm not good enough for you. I know exactly why they invited us here..."

Patrick didn't argue. "Let's just sleep on it, ok? We can talk about it in the morning."

But they didn't talk because Addison had slept on it and the next morning, she called a cab, and didn't look back. She had spent her whole life feeling unwanted, and now that she was an adult, she had a choice in the matter.

"YOU KNOW WHAT I FIND INTERESTING," the deep voice called from the darkness. "That you thought you had a choice in the matter."

Addison wanted to wake up, to open her eyes, to ask what he meant, but she couldn't. She was too tired, too out of it. "Look at you," she heard him say. "You're filthy. No one is going to want you like this..."

The next thing she knew she felt a cool spray hit her skin. It prickled at first, but then the pressure grew. Still, she couldn't open her eyes. She couldn't face him, even if she'd wanted to. "I hope you like water," he said. "By the look of you, the drugs haven't worn off yet." He laughed. "This should help..."

She'd always heard drowning was a quick way to go, now she hoped it was really true.

~

ADDISON FELT like she was drowning without Patrick. They went two weeks without speaking before finally running into each other in the library. Patrick apologized for the way his family treated her. He told her that he was sorry with the way that they had left things and asked her to meet him at his apartment later that evening to talk.

She didn't agree but she didn't tell him no, either. The truth was, she'd been a complete mess since walking out on Patrick. She couldn't eat, couldn't sleep, couldn't do anything but think of him and wonder if she'd done the right thing. Jessica tried to cheer her up by ordering takeout and renting sappy movies but none of it worked. She worried that Addison might be content just sitting around in her pajamas forever, staring into space. In a matter of a week, she had become different, lifeless. She'd only gone to the library because she had to return a book; she couldn't afford the late fees.

Jessica walked over, flipped the TV off, and pulled the covers out from around her.

"Get up," she ordered. "The shower is running. And you know how I hate to waste water."

"What the hell!" Addison said, throwing her hands up. "Since when have you cared about wasting water?"

"Since right now," Jess said tugging at Addison's arm. "GET UP! You'll feel better once you don't smell so bad. Seriously. You can't just lie here forever."

Addison frowned as she searched for the remote. "Maybe I can."

"You've missed classes, Addison. This isn't like you."

"Fine," she said eventually, considering Patrick's offer.

Once showered and dressed, she realized Jessica was right, she did feel better. Also, what could it possibly hurt going over to his place to talk things over?

It was different being in his apartment after everything. Neither of them spoke much, treading carefully, and tiptoeing around feelings like performance artists. It wasn't just that something was different. It was that everything was different.

After dinner they sat on the sofa, Addison sipping her wine, Patrick water. Finally, when she'd had enough of the tiptoeing, when she couldn't take it another minute, she spoke up. "Ok, Patrick. You invited me here. I'm here... so spit it out. I'm a big girl. I can take it."

"Spit what out?"

"Whatever it is you need to say."

Patrick turned toward her, eventually taking her hand in his. He didn't meet her eye. "So . . . Ok . . . I . . . Um . . . I can't do this anymore. Being apart has given me some time to think, and, well, I realized I just don't want anything serious right now. We're *so* young, Addison."

She felt the blow in her stomach. She wanted to cry. But tears wouldn't come. She wouldn't let them. Instead, she put on her best poker face, careful not to give anything away. Knowing that there wasn't anything left to say, she placed her wine on the coffee table and stood, before brushing her hands on her jeans. "Ok," she said, looking back toward Patrick. He grabbed her wrist.

"What are you doing? That's it? All you have to say is ok?" he asked pulling her closer.

Addison wanted to run but she also wanted to stay. The last thing she wanted was for him to see her cry and she knew she needed to make a quick getaway. It was clear that Patrick had made up his mind, and she didn't want to make it any harder for him.

"Come on. Don't run. Please. Let me explain."

Addison felt like a fist was lodged in her throat. "What is there to explain?" she choked out.

Patrick kissed her forehead and then brushed her hair away from her face. Then he leaned in and hugged her so tightly she was afraid she might suffocate. Her mind raced, yet she was numb all at the same time, until it suddenly became clear to her exactly what she had to do.

"You're right and we both know it." She said flatly, pulling back.

Patrick reached for her hand. She looked toward the bedroom. "You don't have to go now," he said, smiling weakly. It was the dimples that made her do it, that's what she'd tell Jessica.

He made love to her gently, as if she might break, as if they both might break. Afterward, he kissed her face and searched her eyes, whispering, "I love you and I'm so sorry," over and over. It tore her apart, literally ripped her heart in two. Still, she didn't respond; instead, she showed him everything she couldn't say without words. When they were both sweaty and emotionally and physically depleted, Patrick curled up next to her, placing his head on her stomach. They lay there staring at the ceiling for hours, neither of them willing to break the silence. Once she was sure Patrick had fallen asleep and she was certain that he was in a deep sleep, Addison got up and silently dressed. After she gathered her things, she stood for a moment watching him sleep. Then she turned and quietly tiptoed out of his apartment and straight out of his life.

~

THE NEXT FEW months were a blur as Addison dated a flurry of men. On the inside, she was devastated. Not only had she lost her boyfriend and lover but her best friend. Her future. On the outside, however, it never showed. "I like my freedom," she'd tell anyone who would listen. "It feels like I'm finally living."

Thankfully, she never ran into Patrick. This wasn't so hard considering she avoided all the places they had gone, places where she thought he might be. In the first few weeks after they split, Addison had received dozens of emails and several phone calls from him. She never answered, deleting the voicemails. It was mostly by mistake she read the first email at all. She'd been drunk, her defenses down. In the email, Patrick explained that he loved her but that his parents had threatened to cut off their financial support if he continued seeing her. He apologized, saying that he would do anything if she would just talk to him. He told her how much he missed her and their friendship. *Fuck him. She had enough friends.* She deleted it without responding. Once, when she was out, Patrick stopped by hoping to see her. Apparently, Jess gave him a piece of her mind in such a way that Patrick finally stopped trying.

During that time, she threw herself into her schoolwork and spent all of her free time bouncing from party to party. It was only after the party that the truth would show, and usually it was Jessica who had to clean up the mess.

After about the twelfth or so guy Addison casually "dated," she met Carter. Carter: rugby player, a typical jock. He was well-known for keeping his life commitment free and

Addison wanted nothing more. They met at his fraternity's kegger and had a one-night stand, of which she remembered very little. Afterwards, he called incessantly, but Addison wanted nothing to do with him. Her heart was broken, and she wasn't looking to date, especially not someone like Carter. Hell, in the daylight, she didn't even like him. But Carter was relentless and she was lonely, and before long the two of them wound up spending a lot of time together, mostly in bed. Or wherever, really. Carter was 'Mr. Fun' 'Mr. Help Her Forget.' He was gorgeous and crazy about her. Which was too bad because Addison knew she would never, could never, love him.

About three months in to "dating" Carter, they bumped into Patrick at a party. He waltzed right up to her and Carter, interrupted their conversation and introduced his date, Shelly. *Some nerve.*

The four of them made awkward small talk until Addison excused herself to the ladies' room. Unbeknownst to her, Patrick followed. He pushed open the stall door and found her leaning against the wall, panting, trying to catch her breath.

She rolled her eyes and attempted to close the door, pushing against it to no avail. Patrick was stronger than she was by a long shot. "What the fuck?" she asked. "You can't be in here."

Not budging, Patrick glared at her, his eyes dark. "Are you happy with him?"

"Ha! How about nice to see you. How have you been? But no. *This* is where you want to start?"

"Addison, answer me. Are *you* happy?"

She crossed her arms, glaring at him before finally speaking. "What fucking business is it of yours?"

Patrick laughed.

She stared at the floor, unwilling to give him the satisfaction of seeing her cry. He pushed his way further into the stall, locking the door behind him. For a moment they just stood there staring at one another, and before Addison could say anything, Patrick grabbed both sides of her face and fell into her, kissing her deeply. He tasted like beer and peppermint and regret. Soon, hands were everywhere. Patrick pushed her skirt up, lifting her slightly, forcing her back up against the wall as he slammed into her. They were drunk and it was sloppy when he pushed into her hard and fast. She dug her nails into his back, which only made him push harder. When he was finished, he slowly pulled away.

Breathless, he bent down and kissed the top of her head. "Fuck, Addison. I've missed you so much."

She smoothed her skirt, trying to gain composure. She refused to let herself get hurt again. "Look, this . . .this was a mistake."

Patrick searched her eyes. "Are you drunk?"

She lied. "No. Why?"

"Let's go."

"Go? Where?"

Patrick unlocked the stall. "Out of here."

She stepped out as Patrick grabbed her by the arm. "We need to go out the back way. I don't want to deal with Carter."

She frowned, rubbing her arm. "What about Shelly?"

"Who?" he asked with a chuckle.

She punched his forearm. "Your date, asshole."

Patrick took her by the hand, intertwining her fingers in his, and ushered her toward the exit. "Oh *her*. She'll be fine."

THE NEXT MORNING, Addison woke up alone in Patrick's bed, angry with herself. The sharp pain of regret hit her right in the solar plexus. After all she had been through only to wind up back here.

She checked her phone. Six missed calls and two voice-mails, all from Carter. *Shit.*

"Good morning, sunshine." Patrick called, pushing the bedroom door open with his foot, interrupting her thoughts in the process. "Coffee?" he asked, thrusting a tray in her direction. He sat down beside her.

"Thanks," she said, sliding upwards into a sitting position, taking the cup from his hands.

As she lifted the mug to her lips, Addison noticed something in Patrick's face change: a thought, a look, something she couldn't place. She took another sip of her coffee as he slid off the bed slowly.

She picked up a piece of bacon and took a bite before realizing what it was he was doing.

Seeing him there, kneeling on one knee, holding the little blue box caused Addison to choke. She tried taking another sip of coffee. Finally, clearing her throat, she laughed and waved him off, but Patrick didn't budge.

"Addison, will you marry me?"

She blinked to make sure she was seeing what she was seeing and then pinched herself for good measure.

Patrick pinched her, too.

"Ouch."

"You're awake," he said smiling. "And— I asked you a question."

Her hands flew to her mouth then. "You're serious?"

"Of course, I'm serious. I was dumb enough to lose you once and I'm sorry for that. But I'm smart enough to know that I don't want it to ever happen again. So... what do you say? Will you marry me?"

So many things ran through her mind in that moment: the how, when, and where, but most of all, the what-ifs. Still, she knew she couldn't let him go, not again. He loved her, he *wanted* her, and that was everything.

"Yes," she replied as hot tears spilled out, stinging her cheeks. "I'll marry you." The rest they would figure out. They had to.

CHAPTER FOUR

Unlike most brides to be, planning a wedding didn't stress Addison one bit. After all, she had hers planned by the time she was six. And as it turned out, things didn't change so very much between the time she was six and twenty-five.

As Patrick waltzed Addie across the dance floor, she smiled and thought to herself: *With a wedding as perfect as this, how could the life together that followed not be just so?* She hadn't yet fully understood, not in the way that you can until you're in the thick of it, anyway, that weddings aren't exactly representative of everyday life. *He won't always look at you this way. You will go days, sometimes weeks like ships passing in the night before you get to the other side. Your wedding day is a dressed up, shined and polished version of what married life is like.* But, of course, no one told her that, and in any case, she probably wouldn't have believed them if they had.

That's not to say she and Patrick weren't happy. It was just different than she'd expected was all.

And then just as it seemed they'd found their rhythm, everything changed. It was almost two years to the day they married that Addison gave birth to their first child; a son they named Connor. While the baby wasn't exactly a surprise, she and Patrick had discussed Addison going off of the pill and trying for a baby, it was safe to say that neither of them expected it to happen so very quickly. Patrick would have preferred a few more years without children, he'd made it clear he wanted to focus solely on his career, which was one reason she wanted a baby in the first place. She wanted him home more and when Addison wanted something, she was persistent.

It was also safe to say that they were both wholly unprepared for the drastic changes that becoming parents would bring to their lives. Addison had planned on continuing on at her job after the baby arrived, and for the first six months following a six-week maternity leave, she did just that.

Unfortunately, her plan didn't last long. Connor was a colicky infant who cried constantly. He rarely slept, and when he did, it was rarely longer than a half-hour stretch. Addison paced the halls with Connor at all hours while he screamed and screamed non-stop. She wore the carpet thin, walking back and forth. *Back and forth.* She found relief in going to work everyday just to get away from the crying. Plus, at work there was a beginning and an end but at home it was just one long stretch of more of the same. There were endless doctor appointments followed by visits to various specialists, who all seemed to confirm what the last had said. Connor was perfectly healthy. Some babies just cry more than others.

There were numerous calls to Jessica during that time in which Addison seemed desperate but swore was all that kept her sane.

"I just need to know it won't always be this way…" she said. "Please tell me, Jess, say it won't."

"It won't."

"They say he's fine. The doctors . . . I just don't get it, though. They're freaking doctors, and they can't give me an answer. Something is wrong. And I haven't a clue what. Aren't mothers supposed to know these things?"

"Did they give you anything to try? What about his formula?"

"We've tried a dozen brands. The way they say to do and nothing... All the doctors tell us the same thing—that he'll grow out of it. But I don't know. Maybe it's me? I'm obviously doing something wrong."

"What does Patrick say?"

"Patrick who?"

Jess laughed.

"He's never home. And really, how can I blame him? I don't think he likes me much, either."

Jessica sighed. She could hear the loneliness in Addison's voice. "Honey, it's not you. It will get better. And if the doctors say he's fine, then believe them. You're a great mother, Add— anyone can see that. Connor is fine. You just need to stop worrying so much. I mean, he is *your* son after all. Remember how much you cried in college? Every twenty-eight days or so."

Addison laughed. "I didn't cry that often."

"Well, you certainly cried more than I did, and that's saying something."

"Thank you," she said.

"I didn't do anything..."

"You listened, you always listen. And you know just what to say to talk me down from the ledge."

"It's nothing."

"It's not nothing—," Addison murmured. Jessica could tell she was crying. "I was beginning to really question my sanity. No one told me how hard this was going to be, Jess. No one said it was going to be so all consuming. He's eight pounds wet, and he's taken over my entire life. And the screaming, I don't know… sometimes I understand how a parent could physically harm their child. Not that I ever would—but I get it. And that's fucking scary. This is my life now," she said. "Everything is different…"

THEY WERE on their fifth nanny in just six short months and that's not including the time Addison took off for maternity leave. By the time Addison hired nanny number six, she began to wonder if word had gotten around. It was becoming increasingly more difficult to get someone to accept the position. When she'd finally succeeded and was able to return to work, it was just two short days before the nanny quit, citing Connor's endless crying.

Patrick came home from work, late again, always late, to find the baby screaming in his crib and Addison lying on the bathroom floor sobbing. "What's wrong?" he asked, but his tone was flat. He was tired, too. "What are you doing in here?"

She didn't answer, not immediately. Eventually, he asked again.

She looked up at him. "The nanny quit."

He frowned. "Ok?"

"Ok?"

"I mean, what else is new? We'll just hire another one."

"OK!" Addison shouted over the baby's cries. "Ok? That's all you have to say? Look—I'm exhausted. I can't even put him down for two seconds, Patrick. And then you say, *we* have to hire someone new, when what you really mean is *I* have to hire someone new. I've missed so much work already. You should see my desk. It'll take me months to get caught up—if ever."

Patrick shrugged and turned toward the door. "You're the one who wanted a kid."

Addison felt the rage building; she felt her face grow hot. "Fuck you."

He turned and walked out. "I'm going for a run. Clearly, we should talk about this when you're not so emotional."

Addison picked up the closest thing to her, a hairbrush, and hurled it at the door, just as he slammed it shut.

IN THE END, Addison hired nanny number seven, an elderly woman named Sue. Sue assured her she could hack it, she'd raised more children than she could count. Unfortunately, by the time Addison found herself back in the office, many of her big projects had been handed off to her colleagues.

Addison couldn't blame her boss, not really. She was a mess. Not just mentally, hopelessness spilled over into every area of her life. Her appearance had become pale and sickly, and her hair was falling out. She had trouble focusing; and it wasn't just the lack of sleep. Her mind was cloudy. She wondered if she might be suffering from postpartum depression; although, it really didn't matter one way or the other. Even if she were, she would never admit it, not to herself and especially not to anyone else.

The harder it became to hold it all together, the more Patrick demanded that Addison leave her job permanently. At first, the conversation occurred weekly until Addison stopped talking to him all together about what was on her plate, after all she knew what he would say. Eventually, it came up daily. "I just don't understand," he would say. "My mom never worked, and I turned out pretty good, don't you think? It's not like we need the money... so what's the big deal?"

"The big deal is that I want to work. But more than that, I don't want to become *your* mother."

He crossed his arms. "What's wrong with my mother?"

"Nothing, Patrick. Nothing is wrong with her. As you can see, she raised such an understanding, intuitive man."

"Good then," he sighed, grabbing his things from the table. "It's settled."

"It's not settled."

He turned back, glancing over his shoulder. "You know, it's amazing how difficult you can be. It's no wonder the baby cries all the time. His own mother would rather go to some low paying job every day, where she's not even really wanted, rather than hang out with him. Have you even stopped to consider how lucky you are? How many women would kill to be in your shoes?"

"It must have slipped my mind," she said and watched him walk out the door. He didn't come back for two days.

She lasted exactly two months before she finally gave in to Patrick's demands. It wasn't that she'd wanted to. Sue quit just like the others and Addison didn't have it in her to try and find a replacement. Not again.

Patrick assured her that she would feel better without the pressure to 'do it all.' On one hand, she thought that maybe Patrick was right. She did feel a ton of pressure. She couldn't cope at work and she was hardly coping at home. Also, by this time several of her friends had also become mothers. They'd chosen to stay home and seemed quite happy with their choices, assuring Addison they wouldn't have it any other way. So, she gave her notice and tried not to look back. She was afraid that if she did, she couldn't stomach the reflection staring back at her.

ONCE ADDISON QUIT HER JOB, she threw herself in to mother-hood. She was consumed by it, and she found that Patrick was happier. Connor seemed to be coming around as well, finally turning in to a chubby little thing that cooed and even smiled on occasion. While he cried less, he still cried *a lot.* There were days when she found herself laying Connor in his crib during one of his screaming fits and walking outside. She'd sit on the front porch for so long that sometimes she couldn't be sure how long she had stayed out there. It could have been minutes or it could have been hours. Time seemed inconsequential. The days dragged on, bled from one to another, all of them exactly like the one before. Minutes gave way to hours and the hours into days and entire months flew by before Addison could question where they'd gone. Mostly, she spent her time wondering how she could fail at some-thing that was supposed to be innate. *Who failed at mother-hood, anyway? Why* couldn't she love being a mother the way her friends did? Still, she said nothing. Not to them, and not to Patrick. She endured and smiled through her unhappiness, all the while, somewhere deep down, she could feel some-thing stirring. And that something was a promise. Albeit a small one at first, she promised that she'd never let herself become *this* invisible again.

Thankfully, somewhere around Connor's first birthday, things gradually started to shift. He started sleeping for six hours at a stretch, which allowed Addison to finally get some uninterrupted sleep. He started walking more and crying less. She became happier too, finding little pieces of herself again. Patrick was as married to his career as ever, but you could tell that, as Connor was becoming more of a little boy, he found it easier to interact with him. Sometimes on Satur-days, Patrick would take Connor to breakfast leaving Addie with almost a half a day to herself. She cherished those hours until she realized she didn't even know how to be alone anymore and eventually she started tagging along, too.

It was also around this time that she and Patrick started communicating again. Now that Connor was doing so many new things each day, there was more to discuss. It was also around this time that the sex life that they both had once enjoyed so much, the glue that had always held them together, started to come back. Slowly but surely, they became a couple again and, with that, a family—the kind of family that Addison had always wanted.

ADDISON HAD MADE up her mind that she was done having children, at least for a very long while, and while she didn't discuss her decision with Patrick or anyone else, Connor was still pretty young and so it rarely came up.

So, a year later, when she woke up dizzy and vomiting, she didn't think, not even for a minute, that she might be pregnant. In fact, it was Patrick who suggested it.

"Nah," Addison reminded him. "There's no way. We've been using protection…"

"Um, yeah, except for that one time that we didn't," he reminded her with the shit-eating grin she both loved and hated.

Fuck. Fuck. Fuck. "What one time?!"

"You know, last month, in the parking garage, after my company party."

"Wait," she said, gripping her temples. "I thought we did…"

He rolled his eyes. "Nope."

"What do you mean nope?"

He shrugged. "I don't carry condoms around with me everywhere I go."

She stood and paced the room. "I hardly remember that."

"You were pretty drunk."

She pinched the bridge of her nose, feeling faint.

"Thanks for letting me know how memorable I am," he called over his shoulder as he walked out, slamming the door behind him.

～

THE NEXT MORNING when Addison peed on the stick, much to her dismay, two bright blue lines quickly appeared.

She stormed out of the bathroom and over to the bed where Patrick was still sleeping. As she sat on the edge of the bed and stared down at him, he stirred and rolled over, peeking his eyes open "What time is it?" he asked groggily.

"Five thirty," she told him with a heavy sigh.

"Why are you up?"

"Because it turns out you were right."

Patrick rubbed his eyes. "Isn't that usually the case?" he asked and then rolled to face her. "What am I right about this time?"

"This," she said, shoving the test into his chest.

He sat up and glanced down at the stick. "You don't seem very enthusiastic.

"I'm not."

He furrowed his brow. "It's not as if we'd planned to stop at one."

"I guess it's just the timing. I'm not ready... I was actually thinking about going back to work next year with Connor turning three and all. Plus, we had such a hard time with *him.* What if this one turns out the same way? Or worse?"

"Bad luck never strikes twice."

She swallowed hard.

Patrick cocked his head as though he'd just remembered

something. "Seriously? This is the first time I've heard you talk of returning to work. I thought we had come to an agreement and put all that behind us?"

Addison stood and shook her head. "Doesn't matter now."

"Well," he said. "I, for one, am over the moon. Connor is going to love being a big brother."

She smiled, but mostly she prayed he was right about this, too.

THREE WEEKS LATER, Addie found herself sitting in the sterile waiting room of her doctor's office, nervous for a reason that she couldn't quite put her finger on. Perhaps, it was just that Patrick was running late. Something had caught him up at the office, which wasn't the least bit surprising. Things at work had ramped up for him and with the excessive nausea she was experiencing, it couldn't possibly have happened at a worse time.

When Patrick opened the door, she saw him before he spotted her. He was rushed, searching the faces for hers. There was so much love in that look, she couldn't help but forgive him.

"Sorry I'm late," he said kissing her cheek. "I didn't miss anything, did I?"

"No, the doctor is running behind due to a delivery. But they should be calling us back soon."

He glanced at his watch. "How long do these things usually take?"

Addison shrugged, twisted her mouth and looked away. Patrick scrolled through his phone.

A few minutes later, the nurse called her name.

In the exam room, Addison changed into a paper gown the nurse had laid out for her and hopped up on the table.

"Earth to Patrick," she repeated twice before he finally glanced up.

"Sorry— I just have to answer a few emails. Things are crazy back at the office."

"Must be pretty important because I was just naked and you didn't even notice."

He laughed. "You're wrong about that. I was watching from the corner of my eye."

Addison adjusted her position. She hated paper gowns and doctor's offices and come to think of it, men. "Why did you come? It's like you're not even here…"

Patrick sighed, stood, and walked over and kissed her head. "Don't be nervous. Everything will be fine."

Easy for you to say, she almost said. But she was interrupted by a knock at the door. Dr. Pierce walked in, followed by the nurse who wheeled in an ultrasound machine.

"Well, hello," the doctor said boisterously. "When I saw you on my schedule, I was a bit surprised. You didn't mention trying for another when you came in for your annual a few months ago… I would've started you on prenatals."

Addison shrugged her shoulders and smiled.

Dr. Pierce instructed her to lie back and then squirted the cold gooey gel on her abdomen. She placed the ultrasound wand, moving it around just a bit. Patrick stood next to Addison, stroking her hand. She looked up at him and then back at the screen. What she saw caused her to gasp. Patrick squeezed her hand. Addison's free hand flew to her mouth. She didn't take her eyes from the screen, registering what she was seeing just as Dr. Pierce did.

There they were. Two blurry blips up on the screen, each tiny dot flickering with a heartbeat. "Twins," Addison said weakly, afraid she was going to pass out.

"Congratulations!" Dr. Pierce said with a chuckle.

"Twins?" Patrick asked, looking back and forth between his wife and the doctor in a way that told them that he wasn't privy to what they were seeing on the screen.

"Oh, my God." Addison cried.

Dr. Pierce went on to give Addison instructions, of which she heard very little. She got dressed, and then she nodded as though she'd heard every word, and took the paperwork that was handed to her. But the room was spinning, and yet at the same time everything was happening around her in slow motion, all at once. Her face grew hot and chills washed over her. She collapsed just as Dr. Pierce and Patrick moved in to break her fall.

CHAPTER FIVE

In hindsight, those two bright blue lines that Addison was surprised to see on the pregnancy test would prove to be very foretelling. She gave birth to twin boys exactly six months later.

Life flew by quicker than ever. After two years at home with her children, Addison decided everyone was ready and since Connor was off to kindergarten, the timing felt right for her to return to work. The truth was, although she'd only ever really admitted it to Jessica, she craved something more. While she loved her family dearly, she had grown tired of feeling bored and unfulfilled. Her days at home were all consuming and yet still mindless and she found herself desperate for something new, anything, to make her feel alive again. Knowing how Patrick felt about her going back to work, she decided it was best not to discuss the matter with him until she found a job.

She hired a professional to tweak her resume, and thankfully it didn't take long for her phone to start ringing. A few weeks after she started her search, she'd landed two interviews. While the first one had been mostly a disaster, she learned a few lessons and felt better prepared for the second.

The morning of her second interview was hectic, trying to get everyone where they needed to be. But she felt ecstatic at the thought of adult conversation, at the thought of being useful to someone other than those who lived in her home.

So ecstatic that she found herself unable to sleep the night before, so she got up an hour earlier than she'd planned and worked out to help keep her calm. Afterward she dressed in a black pencil skirt, crisp white button-down top and peep-toe black pumps, she checked herself in the mirror and asked Patrick if she looked the part.

"You look like a school teacher," he said.

"A teacher? Really?"

"Not just any teacher," he said pulling her close. "The kind you see in one of those low budget adult films."

She pulled away and slapped his arms. "Nice," she said and then she frowned. "Why would you even say that?"

"I'm kidding. You look fine."

"I'm just surprised it still fits after three kids," she said after sweeping her blonde hair up in to a loose bun, hopeful that would make them take her seriously.

"Hair up? Or down?"

"Up," Patrick says. "It makes you look stern. Like a schoolteacher should."

"I'm not applying to be a teacher."

"Or a porn star," he said.

"Stop. You're not funny."

"I'm just saying... you've kept this whole thing very hush-hush. We never discussed you going back to work."

"I didn't know I'd get a call back so fast. I thought I'd just throw my resume around and see what happened."

"Because that sounds like a solid plan."

She knew he was angry. She knew she probably should

have told him. But this, this was what she'd wanted to avoid. The scrutiny. The mocking disguised as jokes.

"What are you interviewing for anyway?"

"A placement coordinator for a staffing agency."

"Sounds easy enough."

"Let's hope."

"Just make sure to mention all of your experience hiring nannies around here, surely they'll hire you then. Look how well that turned out in the end."

"You're an asshole, Patrick."

"What?" he asked, throwing his hands up. "It's true."

ADDISON DROPPED Connor off at school, and waded through traffic on the twenty-minute ride to Jessica's house. Thankfully, Jess had agreed to watch the twins while Addison interviewed.

When she arrived in front of Jessica's colonial, Jess and her two children were watering flowers in the massive front yard as she pulled up. Jess caught her eye and she smiled thinking how lucky she was to have a friend like her. Also, she wished with the slightest bit of envy that she could be as happy as Jess was. Jessica was such a patient mother, the kind who did daily arts-and-crafts projects with her children—the kind who still made homemade Halloween costumes and cookies from scratch. Addison knew that no matter how hard she tried she would never be that kind of mom.

"Thank you so much for taking them for me," Addison said kissing Jess on the cheek. "You're a lifesaver."

"Yeah, well, it was a dumb thing to do saying yes...I don't know what I'm going to do if you get this job. Who will I call and bug all day?"

"You can still call me."

"Yes, but it won't be the same. Now, you'll have a real excuse for not picking up," Jessica said and then she winked.

Addison eyed her boys who'd already run off to find shovels. She bit her lip. "I've gotta run."

"You sure you don't wanna just hang out here and dig in the dirt?"

"I need this job, Jess."

Her friend smiled. "I know."

Jessica blew her bangs out of her eyes and looked at Addison intently. "You look nice. And you didn't even ask for my help. I'm proud of you. Oh—and—hey before I forget," she said reaching into her pocket. She dug out a small bottle of liquor and handed it to Addison. "Right before you go in, just take one long swig…"

Addison furrowed her brow. "Why would I do that?"

"You know you. You're always so nervous. Just try it. Remember back in college, how I'd tell you to have a shot before we went out because it made you so much more enjoyable to be around."

"I try not to think about it."

"Just try it."

Addison shook her head. "Is this why you're so calm?"

Jess laughed and pulled on her glove. "No, it's the gardening."

"I HOPE YOU LIKE GARDENING," the man told her lifting the trap door. "Because unless you can find a critter or two, you aren't going to be eating for awhile." Addison felt him lift her by the hair. He forced her mouth open with his fingers and stuck the water hose inside. She gulped as quickly as she could but the water came too fast. She needed to drink, she knew she needed water but all she tasted was dirt. It was everywhere—in her ears—in her eyes —everywhere.

Finally, he removed the hose, just in time for the water, for everything, to come back up. She couldn't decide which tasted worse, the vomit, the dirt, or a mixture of the two.

"Now, look what you've done," he said. "You're not worth much like this…"

Addison choked. "Here," he offered. "I found one of your friends."

She squinted trying to see through the mud that was caked on her face. He pried her mouth open. She clenched it shut, grinding her teeth, biting her tongue. But in the end, it mattered little, he won. That day she learned, if you swallow them whole, worms aren't the worst thing one could be forced to eat.

ADDISON PARKED her car in the parking garage and then checked her hair and makeup in the mirror. *Maybe Patrick was right. Maybe she did look like a joke.* Maybe this whole thing was a bad idea. What was she thinking having been out of work for almost a decade that someone would just hand her a job? What was she going to tell them that her expertise fell somewhere in the range of making playdough cakes and arranging play dates? Surely, those are marketable skills. Her stomach churned. She was wasting her time and theirs, too.

Addison glanced down at her skirt but it was the bottle Jess had given her that caught her eye and something within her stirred. It was irresponsible and quite frankly out of character. *But, ah, what the hell?* It's not like they were going to give her the job anyway. What harm was there in taking the edge off, as Jess had put it?

Not much, she decided. She downed the contents of the

small bottle. Vodka. *It doesn't smell*, Jess had said. She chased it with a juice pouch because that's all she found in the car. Suddenly her mouth burned and her head felt lighter. She checked herself once more in the mirror before hopping out and making her way to the elevators. The agency's office was located in a beautiful high-rise building in downtown Austin. As she pressed the button for the thirteenth floor, Addison popped a breath mint and tried to remain calm. *It's just a conversation.* She reminded herself. *What's meant to be will be.*

The doors closed as she checked her phone and texted Jessica.

Addison: I drank it. Now I'm buzzing. How are the boys? Also, I've never told you this before. But I think I hate my husband and I'm pretty sure that's not normal.

Jess: YOU DRANK THE WHOLE THING? OMG. Addison! HAAAA. That's so like you. The boys are fine. Now, break a leg. X

Addison: What about the husband thing?

Addison felt brazen and slightly drunk as she awaited a response.

Jess: I'm afraid I'm the wrong person to ask about normalcy...

Addison frowned and then replied: *What is that supposed to mean?*

She sighed. She hadn't noticed the man in the suit standing behind her until she was stumbling backward into him. It could have been the vodka or it could have been the fact that she hadn't worn heels in a while.

Startled, Addison glanced up and caught the man's eye in the mirrored wall. "I'm sorry," she said, feeling her face redden. "I didn't see you there."

The man seemed amused but he only nodded.

As the elevator started to climb, Addison turned her attention back to her phone, waiting for Jessica's reply.

"Don't you think it's strange how two people can be standing inches from one another in such a confined space and yet hardly acknowledge each other?" the deep voice behind her asked.

She looked up, her eyes meeting his in the mirror.

He didn't wait for her reply. "I've always thought so anyway."

Addison smiled nervously. For the first time, she really took notice of the man. He was tall and very handsome with dark hair, and was dressed impeccably. But it was his piercing blue eyes that struck her most. *Probably gay.* Men that dressed this well usually were.

He extended his hand causing her to turn back toward him. "I'm William Hartman."

"Addison," she said placing her hand in his.

He shook her hand slightly, carefully. "And, no, I'm not gay."

Shit. Had she said that out loud? Addison swallowed nervously, pretty sure she hadn't.

"You're easy to read," he said.

Two can play at this game. "Also heterosexual. Married, in fact."

"I figured as much given the ring on your left hand. But you never know," he shrugged. "Sometimes you're wrong."

Addison checked how many floors they had yet to go. *What the hell? Is this man seriously flirting with me?*

He leaned back, taking her in. He had to admit, she surprised him. Not only was she not amused by his charms but she seemed downright annoyed. This, combined with the fact that she was incredibly attractive and quick-witted, intrigued him that much more. "Well, I'm glad that's settled."

Addison wasn't sure what he meant by his statement; all she knew was that she couldn't wait to get out of this elevator. *And what was taking so long, anyway?* Something about this man made her very uncomfortable, the way he shook her hand made her heart race and her knees weak. It's just nerves, combined with the fact you're stupidly and irresponsibly half-way drunk she told herself, almost thoroughly convinced.

Suddenly the lights flickered as the elevator stalled and then plummeted before finally coming to an abrupt halt. Addison fell backward into the man, hitting her head on the mirror as the elevator jolted. He grabbed her before she hit the marble floor, and held her upright.

"Easy there," he said. "You ok?"

Addison's legs felt like putty. She wiped her forehead. *Ouch.* "Um . . . Yeah. Yeah, I'm fine."

She wobbled as he loosened his grip a little. Dizzy and unable to steady herself, Addison grabbed his arm, taking notice of how big it was and how hard his body seemed as she fell against it. She felt like she could stay there forever. *Stop,* she told herself.

"How about this . . ." he started to say. "Here, let's sit," he then suggested, lowering her to the floor.

She smiled. "Thanks."

The lights flickered again, going out completely until dim fluorescent lights came on overhead.

"Are you ok for a second? I'm going to use the emergency phone."

Her mouth went dry. *Emergency.* She was flustered by the way he looked at her, and quite confused, but managed to nod.

"Do you remember my name?"

She furrowed her brow. "Joe. No... Dan... Oh—that's right it's Thomas."

He pulled back, confusion played across his face. "Are you joking?"

"Of course. Your name is William."

"This isn't the time to joke."

"You said I was easy to read."

He grinned but only sort of. "Yeah, well, that was before you hit your head."

William stood cautiously and picked up the phone. Addison listened as he spoke to security. Without taking his eyes from hers, he listened to whoever was on the other end before speaking again. When he did, his voice was calm and intense. It wasn't so much what he said, it was the way he stood, the way he filled space. She listened as he relayed information on who was in the elevator but otherwise only responded with one-word answers. Addison could tell the news wasn't good.

"Listen, have EMTs standing by. I think she might have a concussion. Also, call my office and have them cancel my meetings."

William set the phone down and kneeled beside her. "Where were you headed? Is there anyone we can call for you?"

She took a deep breath in, unconsciously drawing her hand to her mouth. "To a job interview at The Carlisle Agency."

William nodded, and Addison noticed something shift in his expression, there was a look in his eyes she couldn't place. "Thomas, call Ms. Sheehan and tell her Mrs. Greyer is stuck in an elevator in the building."

Addison couldn't help note the way he abruptly barked orders at whomever was on the other end of the phone. He was arrogant and rude, and yet the magnetism she felt toward him was undeniable.

He hung up the phone and sat down beside her. He was so close she could feel the fabric of his suit on her leg. No matter how confined a space they were in, this was *too close*. He smelled amazing. *Had a man ever smelled this good or was that the liquor talking?* It felt as though all of the air had been sucked from her lungs. She looked on as William ran his fingers through his thick black hair, removed his suit jacket, loosened his tie, and patted her thigh as if he'd known her his whole life. "They'll have us out of here soon." She glared at him, speechless.

He laughed. "You have no idea who I am, do you?"

"Should I?" she asked, trying to hide her disdain. She wasn't that good though. She knew he saw it. One minute she was attracted to him and the next he seemed to know exactly what to say to turn it off.

William eyed her impassively. "Only if you want to."

Caught off guard, she looked away. She stared at her shoes until he gently placed his hand beneath her chin and lifted it. "I'm sorry," he said. "For being arrogant... It's just I'm not much of a fan of being trapped."

Something deep inside her burned, it ached at the sound of his voice, begging to crawl right out. "Me either," she said.

"Can I kiss you?"

"If it would help."

He smiled and shook his head. "It won't," he said, and before she knew what was happening, his lips were on hers, and, for a moment, she was lost. William gathered her in his arms and pulled her closer. As she realized what she'd agreed to, Addison pushed his chest to no avail. Either she was powerless to stop or he was incredibly strong. She pushed again; William released her but didn't take his gaze from hers.

Addison shifted away, smoothing her skirt. "I could have sworn I mentioned I was married," she said, thrusting her left hand toward him.

He grinned at her, clearly amused. "What's that got to do with anything?"

Feeling flustered, she finally noticed how hot it was getting in such a small space.

William's hand covered hers "I'm sorry. It won't happen again."

Addison said nothing and backed away from him instinctively. She pulled herself up to a standing position. Her head ached. The two of them stood silently in opposite corners until, uncomfortable, Addison spoke up. "What a day."

"It's not so bad. It led me to you."

She wanted to hate him for saying that. She wanted to hate him for being arrogant and seductive and most of all, for kissing her and making her feel something. But she didn't hate him.

"I don't think there's anyone else I'd rather be trapped with," he said. "Even if that person doesn't particularly like me. And, usually that's what people fear most, isn't it? Being trapped with a person they don't like."

"You seem to know a lot about confinement…"

He pursed his lips. "You have no idea."

She would never be sure if it was the genuineness of the way he said what he said or the glint of sadness in his eye that led her to cross the tiny space and place herself in his arms. She kissed him with a passion that she hadn't felt in quite a while. He matched her style, kissing her back harder than he had the first time. All at once, they were tangled up in each other, tearing at each other's clothes. William pushed Addison's skirt up and pinned her against the wall with his body. "I don't even know you," she said.

"It's probably better that way," he told her and then he lifted her slightly and searched her eyes for an answer before he pushed himself inside her. She dug her nails into the hard muscles in his back. He bit her lip in return. It was angry sex, the ruthless kind, primitive instinct taking over.

After he climaxed, still inside her, William sank slowly to the elevator floor. He took her down with him. She should have seen it as a sign but she was too busy feeling something else. He kissed her bare shoulder. "Damn…"

She smiled faintly and pulled away gently. "I . . .I . . . I'm sorry."

William reached for her hand, reading her mind. "Don't be. I'm not."

Addison rubbed the back of her neck. *Oh God. What the fuck have I just done?* She had never been unfaithful. Had never even considered being unfaithful. And yet, here she was, stuck in an elevator with this man for less than half an hour and had managed to commit one of the biggest sins imaginable.

Sensing her unease, William squeezed her hand and released it. He traced his finger across her lips, sending chills down her spine. "Don't worry," he told her. "Your secret is safe with me."

She studied his face as though she were trying to keep it there, like a token, a memento of the greatest mistake of her life. She wanted to tuck it away in her mind forever and forget it all at the same time. Looking at him made her stomach turn.

William pulled away, releasing her. "Blame it on the concussion," he suggested nonchalantly. He read her well. "You weren't in your right mind."

Feeling as though she could finally breathe, she straightened her clothes. William stood watching her but he said nothing. Finally, he, too, fixed his attire.

"You're a runner," he said eventually.

"Huh?"

"You're a runner."

"Oh—well, yes," she admitted. "But I'm not that good."

He smiled but it didn't touch his eyes. "Somehow I doubt that."

ADDISON WOKE to a strange man stroking her hair. She blinked rapidly and tried to sit up. And then she remembered who he was and what she'd done. "Addison," he whispered, although his tone was urgent. "Firemen are going to be busting through the door in about sixty seconds."

She panicked.

"You passed out," he said.

She heard the door being forced open and then she felt herself being lifted. They placed her on a stretcher. Addison was dizzy and they were hurling questions at her so fast, *too fast*. There was so much commotion. She searched the faces for William's until finally she heard his voice in her ear. "These men are going to take good care of you."

She blinked away tears until his face came in to view. There were so many things she wanted to say, but the words wouldn't come. He smiled slightly, touched her hair, and then he was gone. She remembered that she'd wanted to hate him. She hated herself instead.

CHAPTER SIX

When Addison awoke in the ER, Patrick was by her side. "Hey there, sleepy head."

She searched his face and wondered, *can you tell what I've done?*

He smiled and she got her answer. "Sounds like you had quite the day."

"Yeah," she said picking at his hospital bracelet, unable to meet his eyes. "You could say that."

He shifted, which forced her to look up. "What were you doing at The Hartman Building, anyway?"

The Hartman Building? Addison stared at him confused. "The *what* building?"

"Downtown, Addison," Patrick said sternly. "What were you doing downtown?"

"I told you I had a job interview."

Patrick's mouth formed a hard line, but he said nothing. Breaking the uncomfortable silence, a doctor appeared.

"How are you feeling?" he asked Addison. He stared at her chart looking up briefly.

"Tired."

He looked at her then. "That's pretty normal with a concussion. The good news is your CT scan is clear."

Addison watched as he leaned against the wall. "But I'd like to keep you overnight just to make sure."

Patrick looked at Addison and waited for her to speak. When she didn't, he nodded his head and took out his phone.

"Do you have any questions?" the doctor asked, glancing at the chart once more.

Addison cleared her throat. "Really, I'm fine. I think I'd feel more comfortable at home, resting in my own bed."

Patrick sighed. "How soon can we get her out of the ER and upstairs? She's staying…"

Addison tried to sit up, a little too abruptly. "That's not your call to make. I said I'm fine."

Patrick stared at the doctor as he spoke, though Addison knew his words were meant directly for her. He was angry, and she knew it. "Doc, clearly after the day's events, my wife isn't thinking clearly. It's evident by the fact that she seems to be having a hard time making sound decisions."

The doctor remained cool, neutral. "Look, all I can do is give my professional opinion, and, from a medical standpoint, I'd feel better if we kept you for observation."

Patrick turned to her, as if to say I told you so.

She laid her head back on the gurney, defeated. "What about the kids?"

"I had my mother pick them up from Jessica's."

"Perfect," she said. But it was a lie.

"So, you're okay with staying?" the doctor asked.

She nodded. *You're full of lies today aren't you?* She felt terrible, sick to her stomach over what she'd done. Oddly enough, she wasn't remorseful in the way that she thought she should be. Even as she lay there in the hospital with Patrick at her side, her thoughts drifted back to the man in the elevator. She couldn't help it. Her mind ran back and forth from the way he kissed her, to the expression on his face as they wheeled her away. Addison knew it was wrong. She had lied by omission not once, but a handful of times today. *I hadn't really been looking. The interview just fell in my lap. No, I haven't had any alcohol in the last 24 hours. Yes, I'm fine. No, it doesn't hurt. Yes, admit me, I'm okay with it.* But those lies were small in comparison. Those she could contain. It was the big one that worried her. That one was like a wild-fire. Burning. Burning. Burning.

ONCE THEY MOVED Addison from the ER to her room, Patrick left to gather some belongings. She told him that she would be fine, that he would sleep better at home, but he insisted, saying there was something important he needed to discuss with her.

While Patrick was gone, Addison checked her cell; a few missed calls and a dozen emails. Two in particular stood out. One was from the agency she was set to interview for.

Dear Mrs. Greyer,

We at Carlisle Agency were very sorry to learn of the elevator malfunction you experienced this afternoon.

At this time, following a very prestigious recommendation from Mr. Hartman himself, we would like to offer you the position of Account Manager here at The Carlisle Agency.

Should you accept this job offer, per company policy, you'll be eligible to receive the following beginning on your hire date:

Salary: Annual gross starting salary of $85,000, paid in biweekly installments by your choice of check or direct deposit

Performance Bonuses: Up to five percent of your annual gross salary, paid quarterly by your choice of check or direct deposit

Stock Options: 500 Carlisle stock options in your first year, fully vested in four years at the rate of 125 shares per year

Benefits: Standard, agency-provided benefits for salaried-exempt employees, including the following:

401(k) retirement account

Annual stock options

Childcare assistance

Education reimbursement

Health, dental, life, and disability insurance

Profit sharing

Sick leave

Vacation and personal days

Your work schedule would revolve around appointments you set: that is to say they are flexible.

Should you accept this job offer, per company policy, you'll be eligible to receive the above beginning on your hire date.

We at The Carlisle Agency hope that you'll accept this job offer and look forward to welcoming you aboard.

Sincerely,
Sondra Sheehan
CEO, The Carlisle Agency
(555) 210-3782

Addison was floored *and ashamed.* William had recommended her, and, just like that, she had the job of her dreams. The salary alone was more than she had ever made before. The flexibility in her hours was a dream come true. She could set her appointments in the morning, which would allow her to pick up the boys from school and be there in the afternoons. *Where was the catch?*

Addison checked her voicemail, the first being a message from Ms. Sheehan, letting her know of the offer awaiting in her inbox and explaining that she looked forward to hearing from her. The second voicemail was a hang up from a number she didn't recognize. She clicked off her phone. Everything else could wait. Suddenly, she couldn't wait for Patrick to get back so that she could tell him her news. She had a job, and it was an offer she couldn't refuse.

PATRICK ARRIVED BACK with flowers and Chinese takeout in hand. Her news combined with his sudden good mood nearly made her forget about the day's earlier events. She decided to put what happened in the elevator behind her for now.

"Are the boys okay? They aren't worried, are they? I should call—"

Patrick cut her off. "My mom says they're fine. I spoke with them briefly, but they were too busy helping Rosie bake cookies to really stop and talk."

She smiled, picturing her boys with Rosie, thinking of how much she liked her.

"Eat while it's hot," Patrick demanded.

Addison picked at her food. She wasn't very hungry. "I have some news…"

Patrick took a bite, grinning. "*You* have news? *I* have news. Big news."

Suddenly, she felt nervous. "You go first."

Patrick's mood shifted slightly. She took a deep breath, analyzing the seriousness of his expression. Nothing could have prepared her for what was to come next.

"So, I've been given a huge assignment at work," he paused and smiled. "And I think it's going to be great for us..."

She exhaled the breath she'd been holding in. "And?"

"And . . . I've been asked to head up our newest division in China."

"China?"

"Yes," he said pressing his lips to one another. "China."

"And this is good—"

"I'll get to start from scratch—do with it what I want— run things the way I see fit. It's a year-long project— but I've given it some thought—a lot of thought, actually— and I think it's perfect."

Addison choked. It felt like someone had knocked the wind out of her.

Patrick studied her face and then handed her a drink. "Well—say something. What do you think?"

"Um. I . . . I . . ." she furrowed her brow. "How long have you known about this?"

"Three weeks. Why?"

"Three weeks" Her eyebrows rose and she swallowed hard. "Three fucking weeks, really? And you're just now telling me about it."

"Yeah. I wanted some time to mull it over and get all of the facts before I ran it by you."

"Wow. We're talking about something that will change our entire lives—and you wanted to mull it over before you ran it by me— as if we're discussing dinner plans or picking up milk at the grocery store?"

Patrick stood and paced the room. "So, you're not happy? Of course, you're not happy. You're *never* happy. Don't you realize what this means for my career? What this could mean for us! Seriously, Addison. That's it? You want to pick it apart and argue over how long I've known?"

She pushed her food away. "What do you want me to say?" she shrugged. "It's a bad idea, Patrick."

"Well, you're going to have to say a little more than that. They need me to give them an answer within forty-eight hours."

"Well then. What more is there to discuss? It sounds to me as though you've already made up your mind... the only thing left to do was to 'run it by me.'"

Patrick moved closer, putting his hand on her leg. "Addison, come on. You know that is not what I meant. You mean the world to me; your opinion means the world to me. Look, I realize this is a lot to take in all at once. But it's only for a year, and I know we can make it work. You and the kids can visit, and I'll fly home as often as I can..."

"It's fucking China, Patrick, not California. You can't just hop on a plane and be home in a few hours."

"Of course, I realize that."

"So..."

"So—opportunities like this only come up once in a life-time. It's what I've been working so hard for. So many of my colleagues would kill for this opportunity, but they asked *me*. Don't you see what this means? It means that I'm closer than ever to making partner. This is what we've always dreamed about."

She opened her mouth and then closed it again. She wanted to tell him he was wrong. That it was what *he'd* always dreamed about. Instead she said, "I don't want you to go, Patrick. I need you here. The *boys* need you here."

"Don't do this, Addison," he said and she could hear the warning in his voice. "It's just a year."

The nurse came in to take her vital signs. Addison and

Patrick stared at each other silently as she charted information. *Who are you*, she thought looking at him. *Who did I marry?* Eventually, it was Addison who broke the uncomfortable silence.

"I guess you've made your mind up, then."

Patrick stood, running his fingers through his hair. "I need some air."

"Wait. I didn't get to tell you *my* good news."

Patrick raised his eyebrows. "Oh. Yeah?"

"I got the job."

Patrick's jaw set as he turned and walked out, saying everything he needed to say by saying nothing at all.

Addison lay there, staring at their cold, uneaten food, listening to the machines beep, and thought about how this morning, when the alarm had gone off, it had been, for the most part, a normal day. And now, here she was lying in a hospital bed after betraying her husband in the worst way. To make matters worse, he just told her that he was leaving their family for a year and he'd known it for weeks. Now, she wasn't sure who had betrayed who the worst. She knew she could tell him not to go. She already had. But Patrick had made up his mind, and it seemed the only option she had left was to issue an ultimatum. But she wouldn't. Addison was smart enough to know that doing so would only lead to a life of regret and what ifs. She did not want to become that to Patrick, which meant she knew exactly what she had to do. What she hadn't expected was just how much it would hurt.

Patrick didn't come back that night. Not that she had expected he would. The next morning he showed up with a bagel and orange juice, which she understood was his way of making amends.

He handed her a cup. "So, I hear you're coming home today."

"Yep," she said taking a sip. "I've been given the all clear. They're finishing my discharge paperwork now."

He glanced at his watch. "I hope they're quick. Tee time is at ten."

"You're golfing today?"

"Yeah, remember? I told you," he said, reaching forward messing up her hair a little. She knew what his gesture meant. That's what being with a person this long does to a person. You memorize for better, or worse, all their subtleties. Patrick was suggesting that hitting her head made her forgetful when really golfing at a time like this just made him an asshole.

ON THE RIDE HOME, they mostly talked logistics, matter of factly. Both of them careful to steer clear of any and all emotion.

"So . . .tell me about this job," Patrick said. "I assume you've decided to take it."

"The hours are flexible and they're offering me $85K a year."

"That's not so much... not when you really think about it. Not when you factor childcare into the equation." He looked over at her then. "Have you? Have you done that?"

"I'm well aware of how much it costs to raise children."

"Not raise them," he corrected. "Babysit them."

"Right."

"Well, it'll all work out, I'm sure."

"And you?" Addison replied. "What have you decided?" she asked watching his profile carefully.

"I leave in two weeks."

Her breath caught. "Two weeks," she repeated, just as soon as the words could form around the lump in her throat. "What about the boys?"

He turned to her then. "That's why maybe this job thing won't be so bad. I mean... okay... admittedly I have no idea why on earth you're not happy at home, why you'd want to go back to work...considering I make a comfortable living... not to mention that a sizable chunk of any income you bring in will go toward someone else raising our kids... I do agree the timing isn't half-bad. They'll be so wrapped up in a new school, a new routine, they'll hardly even notice I'm gone..."

"Of course they'll notice."

"But they're young and resilient. It's not like they see me that much as it is. More often than not they're in bed by the time I get home."

"Tell me something I don't know."

But he didn't. He didn't tell her anything new. *Never get too close to anyone,* her Grandmother always said. *They'll let you down every time.*

~

NEWS of her husband's upcoming departure spread fast. Addison found herself fielding phone calls from friends and family who were curious to find out if the news was true. After a handful or so, she stopped picking up the phone. Only Jess said what she'd really been thinking. *"How can he do this? And aren't you going to fight him on it?"*

"What would be the point?" she'd said. "His mind is made up."

"Cry. Throw a fit. I don't know, something. Being a single mother is hard, Addison," Jess assured her.

"I'm not much of a crier."

Jessica sighed. "It might be a good time to change that. It

doesn't make you a bad person to ask that he stay, you know."

"I can't," she said and she pushed the thought away, burying it deep down, where she was sure it wouldn't come up again.

"I don't understand you," Jess replied. "But more than that, I'm really sorry. I can't imagine."

"I'm fine," she said and then she laughed. "It's just a year."

"I hope so," Jessica told her. "But I remember last time, what happened when the two of you split. I was there, remember?"

"I do remember. And, anyway, it's not like we're divorcing. He was offered a promotion. It just happens to be in another country. Military families do this all the time. But worse. They're actually putting their lives on the line."

"Yes," Jess said. "But you didn't marry anyone in the military. Patrick didn't enlist. He's just being a selfish prick."

"He's trying to make a better life for his family. And as I said, I'm fine with it," Addison replied. But there was a hard edge to her voice when she said it. The kind that could only come with a lie. And lie she did. To anyone and everyone who brought it up. Her friend was right. She hadn't signed up for this. Her marriage was in shambles, so very far from where she'd ever imagined it as she'd said "I do" underneath the willows. The last thing she wanted or needed was to have to comfort others or to continue to explain to them that everything was going to be fine. So, instead she lied. She put on a brave face and she lied. After all, she'd need the practice when it came time to tell her children. When her friends asked, she told them she was excited for what the opportunity meant for Patrick's career.

Perhaps, she told herself, if she repeated it enough, she might even begin to believe it, too.

WILLIAM HARTMAN WAS NOT a patient man. He'd never had to be. An only child, his father had bailed while he was still too young to know any different. Lucky for him, his mother had married well—all five times. Also, she had a type, marrying one Wall Street banker after another, each of them having a range of feelings towards William, which varied from disdain to indifference. He would tell you, of all of them, indifference was the worst.

William attended the best private schools that money could buy and eventually the best boarding school in the country. While he was still at home, he studied his mother's husbands, listening to their conversations and learning all things business. He understood early on that if he intended to get ahead, he'd have to wall himself off, show little to no emotion, and what he did show, well, no one said it had to be real. In fact, it was better if it wasn't. That was how you beat them at their own game. *Second best did not a winner make.* So that's what he did. He played the game and he played it well. He graduated from Harvard, near the top of his class even though he hated school. *They won't take you seriously without an education.* After he'd earned the degree and the right to be taken seriously, he started his business, Hartman Enterprises, in which he began buying up businesses that were on the verge of failing. He bought low and sold high, often dabbling in real estate as well.

William was a natural at knowing what to do, what to say in order to get what he wanted. Soon, he was well known for having one of the best real estate and business portfolios in the United States. By age thirty, he made the Forbes list as one of the world's youngest billionaires. Sure, his personal life was nearly non-existent but he was on top. The rest could be faked. In truth, he had very few close friends, and, while there was no shortage of women in his life, he rarely dated any of them twice. William had a philosophy about mixing business with pleasure, and, since his world revolved around business, he found the philosophy fairly easy to manage.

That is, until the day he met Addison Greyer. For one, he'd pegged her wrong. He hadn't imagined *she'd* be the type to have sex with him minutes after shaking his hand. And when she did, he certainly didn't foresee her refusing his calls or his emails afterwards. That was his game. And he'd never been beaten at his own game.

But then, she rubbed him the wrong way. That was why he told himself he couldn't stop thinking about her. She was rude. He'd gotten her a job and she hadn't even the courtesy to thank him. If there was one thing William Hartman couldn't tolerate, it was poor manners. Had she not broken all of his rules, had she not defied logic, he told himself, he never would've paid it any further attention. But as the days went on and he thought about their encounter, he couldn't get her out of his mind.

He sent her flowers in the hospital and on her first day of work, which she ignored. Only the more she ignored him, the more interesting she became. Women didn't treat him this way, which explained why he was taken aback and all the more intrigued when she did. That was the thing about William, he trusted his intuition, and, when it told him to pursue something, he did.

CHAPTER SEVEN

The days left until Patrick's departure were dwindling down quickly. Addison found herself collapsing from sheer exhaustion each evening, which made it fairly easy to put what she had dubbed "The Elevator Event" out of her mind, despite the fact that William Hartman had called and emailed several times. She hadn't read the messages, instead she forwarded them off to a separate folder to be opened and dealt with later, when things settled down.

Finding a nanny for the twins and dealing with the plethora of changes headed her way made it pretty easy to set everything else aside. It didn't help that she couldn't look her husband in the eye without feeling sucker punched. *Look at what you've done. This is why he is leaving you. Of course, he is. You never deserved him in the first place.*

A week before Patrick was scheduled to leave for China, Addison started her new job. The Carlisle Agency was an upscale placement service, which supplied household staff, everything ranging from a single cleaning lady to full-service staff, capable of managing entire estates. Her job in particular was to interview potential clients, to understand their needs, and then sell them on the agency.

Thankfully, she used the agency to find Kelsey, the nanny, who would care for the boys and considered it beneficial to have gone through the process.

That's not to say it was a completely smooth transition. It took some getting used to, having to be somewhere every day, and overall, getting acclimated to being in an office environment again made her feel a bit out of her league. It all wasn't hard though. She had a corner office, overlooking the Austin skyline. Spacious and contemporarily decorated, and, more importantly quiet, coming to work every day did in many ways feel like a small luxury. Still, there was something about her colleagues that made her a little uneasy. There were ten women in her office and three men. Most of them were a good decade younger than she was and all were attractive enough that they could easily grace the cover of any of the latest fashion magazines. Apparently, the agency only hired beautiful people, which added to her insecurity. *Why am I here,* she often thought, looking around. *I don't fit in.*

ON ADDISON'S second day of work, her boss waltzed into her office and ordered her to follow. She had heard rumors about Sondra Sheehan; mostly that she was a tough boss, one in which caused few people to stick around. Addison followed her into a conference room where she shut the door. Addison eyed the racks of clothing and the small group that stood before her, waiting.

She couldn't help but notice the disdain written on Sondra's face. Next to her, a petite man, Sondra's assistant, cleared his throat. "Honey, there is no particularly nice way to say this, but your style is absolutely dreadful."

Addison cocked her head to the side and studied Sondra, a mixture of annoyance and confusion on her face. *She called her in for this?* Admittedly, she thought she looked pretty good. "I'm not sure what you mean."

Sondra shook her head from side to side and then exhaled loudly. "I knew this one would be trouble."

Javier stepped in. "Look—we just figured you could use some help: a makeover of sorts. Consider it a welcome gift."

Addison shifted her weight from foot to foot and surveyed the room. "Does everyone here get welcome gifts?"

Sondra eyed her intently. "The ones who need it."

"That's really kind," Addison told her. "But I'm pretty sure this is all unnecessary. If there's some sort of dress code I'm supposed to adhere to, I can manage fine shopping on my own."

Sondra slammed her hand against the massive mahogany table. Hard. "For God's sake, Mrs. Greyer. You are in sales. And your taste is shit. Javier may have put it nicely, but I won't. You are a representative of this agency, and you will look and behave like it at all times. Do you catch my drift?"

Addison felt the sting of her words, but determined not to let her emotions show, she simply replied, "Well, when you put it like that, it all makes so much sense. Although— I have to question your judgment a little, seeing that you are the one who hired me."

Sondra Sheehan turned on her heel and left the room just as abruptly as she had entered; Javier gave Addison a look, she knew it well, it was one of warning. Then he turned and followed, trailing Sondra.

Addison could see that she'd irritated her boss. She realized, albeit too late, that she should have just accepted the help, and the clothing, but something in her couldn't;

wouldn't. Which is why it only added to her confusion as she noticed the slightest hint of a smile playing on Sondra's face as she rounded the corner. If Addison hadn't known better, she'd swear that there was a hint of satisfaction in it.

BY THE TIME Patrick's departure date finally arrived, Addison hadn't slept all night long. Not that night and not many before. Instead, she tossed and she turned. She stared at the ceiling. But mostly, she thought of *him.* She thought of that elevator, of those mirrors. She thought about how she avoided that particular one every morning on her way up to her office. Once she even took the stairs. *She deserved to suffer.* She thought of his mouth on hers, his hands on her body. His arrogance. It ate at her. She counted sheep, and when that didn't work, she picked up a book, and when her eyes grew weary, she went downstairs and stepped on the treadmill. *Anything would do. Anything but thinking of him.*

At one point, she considered telling Patrick about the incident, thinking maybe she should come clean. She even came close, opening her mouth before closing it again. She took an apple from the fridge and chewed it slowly, counting each bite, one by one. *Anything to keep the secrets in.*

She would tell him at some point. She had to. Surely, she owed him that much. In the meantime, she considered not telling him and begging him to stay instead. Finally, the morning he was due to fly out, unable to sleep yet again, she drug herself out of bed, went downstairs, and put on tea. After filling her cup, she sat down at the table and opened her laptop, figuring Google might give her an inkling of what to do. She laughed to herself, considering the phrases she might use. *'Husband leaving family for a year'* or *'Wife is a cheater. Should she come clean?'*

Still, her thoughts led her back to William. Maybe it was the fact that she was delirious, emotional and quite frankly when it came right down to it, a little angry, but this time curiosity got the best of her. She opened the folder she'd set up for non-urgent emails to go in to. *Six emails.* She clicked on the first.

From: William B. Hartman
Date: 6/12/12
To: Addison Greyer
Subject: Thinking of you

Dear Addison,

I've tried calling several times with no luck. I wanted to visit you in the hospital, but I thought better of it, not wanting to make matters any worse. I felt a little better knowing that you were given a clean bill of health. Hopefully, you received the flowers I sent: orchids. I hear they are your favorite.

I was wondering if you would like to have dinner. I understand that your life situation may preclude this, but I can't stop thinking of you and was hoping to get to know you a little better. Clothes on this time, I promise.

Sincerely,
William

So that's what he wanted. Dinner. No, thank you. More importantly, how did he know personal details about her life? Especially when she knew so little about him. Sure, she knew that he was some big shot financier who came from a wealthy family. She knew the building she worked in was named after them. But aside from that, and aside from putting in a good word for her, basically landing her a job, in all honesty, she hadn't really thought about him personally beyond that.

She typed his name into Google. Up popped his Wiki-pedia page, complete with a photo. Addison felt a knot form in the pit of her stomach. Those eyes. She remembered that he was gorgeous, but seeing him there on the screen set her back. In the photo, his hair was shorter. He looked younger. As she read up on him, seeing his net wealth laid out before her, she was shocked, not only at his accomplishments but that the building she worked in wasn't his family's. It was *his. Dinner. Of course, he wants to have dinner.* Addison knew the type. At least she thought she did, anyway. *No thank you.* She closed out her browser and shut the screen. *You shouldn't have been so stupid. You think you know his type, well, he certainly thinks he knows yours. To him, you're just another woman willing to spread her legs for him, in hope of hitting the jackpot.* Addison laid her face on the table. She felt humiliated.

"Whatcha doin' down here?"

Addison jumped, feeling Patrick come up behind her, slipping his arms around her waist.

"Damn it," she said lifting her head. "You scared the shit out of me."

Patrick laughed. "Sorry. Couldn't help myself."

"I couldn't sleep," she told him, unable to mask the irrita-tion and humiliation in her voice.

"You should've woken me."

She rolled her eyes. Patrick grabbed her by the hand. "Come back to bed."

Addison did as he asked. After all, things were messed up enough already, what was one more mistake.

ADDISON FINALLY DOZED off sometime before daybreak. She awoke to the sound of her alarm, unsure exactly how long she had been asleep. She looked at the clock, trying to determine how many hours she had before she had to make the drive to the airport. The realization that she had to make the drive at all stung.

Later she would plaster a smile on her face, gather her kids in the car, and drive her husband to the airport to board the flight that would take him halfway around the world. *Away from her. Away from their family. To another way of life. To another time zone.*

It would be almost three months before she would see him again, before the boys would hug his neck again, and it broke her heart. While Connor mostly understood that his father was leaving and that it would be months before he saw him again, Addison knew deep down that, at age seven, he didn't fully grasp the concept of time or the reality of how long his dad would be away. And the twins had no idea. Sure, they knew Patrick was getting on an airplane and would be gone for a while, they were too young to comprehend what this meant. Of course, there would be phone calls, Face Time, and Skype, but it wasn't the same.

Addison had tried to prepare them as best she could. She bought a big calendar and marked the days until Daddy left and until his return.

Soon, sounds of the kids filled the house. She could hear Patrick downstairs talking to them. *Up and at 'em.* She forced herself out of bed, even though it was the last thing she wanted to do—she wasn't ready to face the day. But she pulled herself together anyhow, knowing that she had to get through this day for the boys—to make it as normal as possible for them.

On the way to the airport, the boys did most, if not all, of the talking. "Daddy, where is China?"

Patrick smiled but didn't take his eyes off of Addison. "China is located on the continent of Asia."

She glanced in the rearview mirror where she could see the wheels in her son's mind turning. "What's it like there?"

Patrick smiled. "Well, there are people. Lots of people. And Chinese food."

Once they arrived at the airport, the boys shifted their questions away from China and began fielding questions about airplanes. Patrick continued answering them, but she could see that his heart wasn't in it. He was too busy studying her. It was as though he was taking her in, memorizing her. Whatever it was he was doing, it made her uneasy. She kissed him goodbye quickly and asked the boys to do the same. Their goodbyes were different than she'd imagined all this time. There was little fanfare in the farewell. Addison was afraid that she would crack again, the way she had last night after they'd made love, with little or no warning. And that was the last thing she needed. She'd cried and begged him not to go, just as Jessica had suggested. However, either, she had been right all along— she couldn't make him stay— or it was too little, too late.

⁓

WHEN SHE AND the boys arrived home, the house felt different. *Emptier.* Addison checked her phone. There was a text from Patrick. *Miss you guys already. Check the mudroom.*

She did as he'd instructed, expecting flowers or a small gift. What she found instead was a puppy. That and several piles of shit to clean up. I have to get rid of this, she thought. But it was too late. The boys had come barreling in behind her.

⁓

ADDISON KNEW about the five stages of grief one supposedly

goes though during a major life change: Denial, Anger, Bargaining, Depression and Acceptance. Oddly enough, she seemed to have skipped the first stage and landed herself smack dab in the middle of the anger stage. After all, Patrick was already leaving her with so much responsibility. *What was he thinking leaving a puppy to top it all off?*

"Daddy said he had a present for us," Connor told her, his eyes wild. "I didn't know it was going to be a real live dog!"

She watched as the puppy licked their faces. They squealed. Eventually, she excused herself and went in search of cleaning supplies. Anything to keep them from seeing her cry. She let the tears fall and she let herself hate Patrick for leaving her with a dog; all the while hoping that in time the smiles on the boy's faces would help mend her broken heart.

CHAPTER EIGHT

The following morning Addison walked into the office, feeling numb, depleted, like shit in the worst way. She hadn't slept much in the past few days, and to top it off, the damned puppy had kept her up last night with his whining. Of course it had, that's what puppies do. Finally, desperate, she crawled out of bed, went downstairs, and brought him to bed with her. She knew better, but she also knew she needed sleep if she was going to survive the new single-parent role she'd just been thrust into.

Opening the door to her office, she kept the lights off and quickly closed it behind her. The last thing she wanted was to be bothered today, neither her throbbing head, nor her patience could take it. Dumping her purse and computer bag on the floor, she sent a text to the nanny asking that she and the twins do their best to keep the puppy awake today. The last thing she needed was a repeat of last night.

"Addison," a deep voice said startling her. "We need to talk."

She jumped, the cell phone in her hand hitting the floor with a thud.

"Jesus!"

She turned to see William Hartman sitting at her desk. Dressed in an all-black three-piece suit, he wasn't easy to miss. She took in the sight of him. *Damn.* Something about him was different than she'd remembered. *His hair. Maybe.*

She crossed her arms and leaned back against the wall, using it to steady herself. "What are you doing here?"

William rubbed his jaw, staring silently, as if trying to figure out his response. "You haven't answered my calls or emails, and like I said, we need to talk."

"Um . . . Yeah, about that—"

"The incident the other day in the elevator was video-taped. My team is in negotiations to purchase the tape before it is released to the media. So far, at this point, every offer has been turned down. I just wanted you to know—it's going live in the morning."

Addison's mouth dropped. Bile rose in her throat. Thinking she might be sick, she took a seat opposite William. "What?" She shook her head and then steadied her gaze on him. "How?"

"These things happen."

She frowned and crossed her legs. "That's all you've got to say? These things happen. Well—what in the hell are we going to do about it?"

William took a deep breath. "I'm sorry," he said nonchalantly. "We don't know exactly how they'll spin it, but my PR team has been prepped and is well prepared to handle the aftermath."

She scoffed. "Yeah, well that doesn't exactly help my situation."

He raised his brow. "Look, we'll handle this, ok? We'll work it out."

Addison looked away. Her thoughts raced back and forth between Patrick and her children. *Of course, it would all work out . . . for him.* She'd have to call Patrick and tell him herself, before he found out the hard way. She did at least owe him his dignity. *Then again, maybe he didn't have to find out at all. China is pretty far way.* No, someone would tell him, and it would likely be her disapproving mother-in-law. *"We tried to tell you about that one,"* they'd say.

William stood, walked around to the front of the desk and perched himself there. He reached down and took her hand in his. She swallowed hard. She wanted to recoil, to pull away, but she didn't. *Why did this man have this effect on her?*

"I've arranged for a car to pick you up here at noon. Carl, my driver, will be there waiting for you. He knows who to look for, so just follow him to the car. He and two members of my security team will take you to an undisclosed location. I'll meet you there."

She pulled away then and looked up at him, her eyes narrowed. This was not her life. Sneaking into cars. Drivers. Security. Undisclosed locations. None of it. She wanted none of it.

William spoke firmly then, interrupting her thoughts. "We can't talk here, Addison. It's too risky. We need to talk and sort this out. My guys are good. They'll get you there and back, unnoticed."

She nodded. *Of course, they couldn't talk there.*

William stood and gave her shoulder what she assumed was supposed to be a reassuring squeeze and walked towards the door. Turning back, he paused just before opening it. "Oh, and Addison . . ."

She didn't look at him, she couldn't. There was something about the smooth tone of his voice that unsettled her. "Yeah?"

"You're even more beautiful than I remembered."

Then, just as quickly as he'd come, he was gone.

Many women might have been flattered. Maybe that was what he was going for, but all Addison could think about was what deep shit she was in. Clearly, she hadn't just made a one-off mistake. No, she'd gotten in way over her head.

ADDISON WANTED Patrick to hear the news from her. She owed him that much, and now that she was backed into a corner, she figured there was no time like the present. She dialed his cell, unsure of exactly what she would say, of how she would shatter everything he thought he'd known about the woman he'd married.

He answered on the first ring. "Hey, honey," he said, his tone upbeat. "Funny—I was just thinking about you."

Fuck. The sound of his voice threw her off and just like that she'd almost lost her nerve. She stayed silent for a moment, listening to voices in the background. "Where are you?"

"The team and I are just leaving a meeting only to head to another. Hang on a sec—"

Addison heard him speak to someone in the background about logistics.

"Sorry about that," he told her, coming back on the line. "I've only just arrived— and already it's never ending."

"I'm sure," she said, and she could hear the tension in her tone.

"How are the kids?"

"They're great," she told him blinking back tears.

There was more chatter in the background. "Sorry," he said. "The Chinese don't know much of privacy, it seems. Well, that and it's so crowded here. You wouldn't believe it…"

"What were you thinking?" Addison asked.

"Coming here? It's not all—"

"No," she said cutting him off. "You said when I called that you were thinking of me…"

"Oh, you know. The usual. Like how I can't wait to see you again—how much I'm looking forward to coming home...."

"Hmmm..." was all she could get out. "But Patrick—I was wondering... what if—"

"I'm coming," she heard him say.

"Sorry. What were you saying?"

She winced. "What if we can't make this work?"

Dead silence.

"Patrick?"

She heard him sigh. "Of course we can make this work."

"Yeah—but what if—"

There was a lot of commotion in the background. "Shit," Patrick said cutting her off. "I'm sorry. I've gotta run. They're waiting on me," he sighed. "Can I call you tonight?"

As she hung up the phone, Addison laid her head on her desk and let the tears come. Her head was spinning. She'd had the chance to tell him, the chance to come clean her way, and she'd blown it. There was no doubt, this would end her marriage. Patrick was not the kind of man who could forgive this kind of betrayal. It wasn't just the big lie that would do her in, but all the small ones, too. She thought of her children growing up going back and forth from one parent's home to another's, never feeling like they quite belonged in either one. That's what this would do to them and it was entirely her fault. There was no denying that. Her children would never forgive her. This realization only made Addison sob harder.

"Uhhmm," a voice said, startling her. *Well, that's two times today.* When she looked up and found her boss staring at her disapprovingly, she was certain the day couldn't get any worse.

"Everything ok, Mrs. Greyer?" Sondra asked, eying her quizzically.

Addison searched her desk for the box of tissues. "Yes," she said. "Sorry," she added sitting up a little straighter. "Just having a rough day."

Sondra moved closer. "Would this happen to have anything to do with Mr. Hartman?"

Addison froze. *Shit.* "Who?"

"Look, Mrs. Greyer, I'm not going to waste your time here. And I'm going to ask that you don't waste mine. Are we clear?"

Seriously. "I'm afraid I don't know what you mean," Addison said, feigning ignorance. It was the best way to tell a lie without outright having to do it.

"I know what happened in the elevator, Addison."

Addison's face remained neutral, refusing to give anything up. "The elevator?" *Make her spell it out. Do not let this woman, boss or not, get the best of you.*

Sondra shoved papers and a sealed envelope she'd been holding onto Addison's desk. "I need you to sign the top form."

Addison glanced at the paperwork in front of her and back at her boss. "But I signed a confidentiality agreement in my new-hire paperwork."

Sondra frowned. "This one is different. It's personal. You need help. Here is my offer," she said, pausing to sigh loudly. "Sign the goddamn paper, Addison."

Something in Sondra's tone, something in the way that she looked at Addison, told her what she knew she needed to do. She signed the form and pushed it back across the desk.

Sondra nodded and then pressed her lips to one another before speaking again. "Read the proposal and see me in my office tomorrow morning, eight o'clock sharp. And remember, you signed the agreement, Mrs. Greyer. No one's eyes but your own are to view what's inside that envelope, are we clear?"

"Clear as day," Addison said.

"Good," Sondra replied. "Now, are you sure you don't want to discuss your predicament?"

Addison narrowed her gaze. "My what?"

"Nothing."

"Sondra?" She watched as her boss turned.

"Close the door behind you on your way out, will you?"

Sondra turned and waltzed out, slamming the door behind her. She had to admit she *really* liked this girl. She could see that this was going to work out well. *Very well, indeed.*

DESPITE EVERYTHING ON HER MIND, Addison managed to set three appointments before she was due to meet with William. She glanced at the clock and realizing that she needed to be downstairs in half an hour, she thought it would do her good to freshen up. *Why should I even care?* She was bothered by the fact that she wanted to look good for William. Stalling, she checked her email one last time. There was an email from William. Her breath caught. She hated that he had this effect on her. She clicked to open it anyway. *Never show up to a meeting unprepared.*

From: William B. Hartman

Date: 6/16/12

To: Addison Greyer

Subject: Impatiently waiting . . .

Dear Addison,

Mere words cannot describe how it felt seeing you again this morning. I never could've imagined it possible to miss someone this much. Someone I barely know.

I am beyond sorry that we have found ourselves in this situation. I never intended to hurt you. It pains me that my celebrity has encroached upon your life, and I promise to do everything within my power to see that you and your family remain in anonymity.

That said, I do believe that sometimes events can occur in our lives that lead us down a different path than the one we thought we were on: a path that steers us in a new direction. While we may not have intended to take this route to begin with, here we are. I have no doubt this path will lead us to bigger and better places, to dreams we didn't know we had.

Yours,
William

P.S. Make sure you delete this immediately after reading it. Then, empty your trash, so it's not stored there.

Addison exhaled. *What path was he referring to? The only one she was concerned with was her certain path to divorce court and the long slow road to hell after that.* She was in trouble—big trouble. Grabbing her purse, she headed down the hall to the ladies' room. Looking in the mirror, she realized that if she hadn't known better she could easily pass for someone on her way to a funeral. The little black dress and peep-toe pumps were certainly fitting for a day like today. Once she'd washed her face and reapplied her makeup, she hurried down to the lobby. Although it was buzzing with people, it didn't take her long to spot Carl. He'd obviously noticed her before she had him, and once she met his gaze, he nodded quickly, ushering for her to follow where a black SUV was waiting just outside at the curb.

No sooner had she hopped in than the door was closed behind her. Addison couldn't help but feel intimidated by the three large men in suits who occupied the car with her. She nodded slightly, as if to say hello but remained quiet the rest of the ride. She strained her ears, trying to hear the conversation between the two men in the front but only garnered bits and pieces, mostly about whether or not they were being trailed.

They pulled into a parking garage of The Plaza. *Why were they at The Plaza? They were supposed to be going to an undisclosed location. Everyone and their mother knew where The Plaza was.*

Carl opened the door for Addison, ushering her out. He seemed to sense her confusion. "Slight change of plan."

Addison studied the man briefly. She shook her head, then a shrug of solidarity. *If you say so.* He led the way, she followed. The other men did, too.

They made their way into the elevator, where she watched him press a button marked "P". As the elevator climbed, she also noticed that everyone with the exception of Carl was unwilling to look her in the eye. "Well, you're certainly a friendly bunch. Not from Texas, I assume."

The men didn't reply. But they did nod and they did look her in the eye for the first time. The shorter one even smiled a little.

The elevator door opened to a large foyer. Her throat seized just a little at the sight of William standing there in his dark pressed jeans and white t-shirt. She didn't know what she'd expected. But it wasn't that. For one, he looked younger dressed like this. The men who had accompanied her suddenly made themselves scarce.

"Welcome to my home," William said. He smiled but it didn't touch his eyes.

She scanned the palatial high-rise apartment. It was notably gorgeous with its exposed stone, luxurious oversized leather sofas, and antique, yet homey, feel. "Why am I here?"

"I thought we'd clarified that already…"

God, he was so condescending. "Nope," she replied crossing her arms. "I thought you said we were meeting at an undisclosed location, and you bring me to your goddamned house! Is this all some sort of joke to you, William?"

"Whoa. Easy there. No, actually it's not some sort of joke. In fact, it's cost me a fair amount of time, and well, the money part is no joke either—if you must know."

"Nice."

"Look," he said. "I'm sorry. I . . . This . . . Well, I wanted to tell you… My attorneys managed to stop the sale of the tape. Though to be honest, we're not sure for how long." He let out a long slow sigh. "It may be only temporarily."

Addison walked over to the floor-to-ceiling windows, trying to put as much space between the two of them as possible. "This—" She lowered her voice. "This is my life we're talking about. I have a husband and children—a family —people who count on me. And I let them down. Majorly."

From her periphery, she watched as William sat on the oversized couch in the middle of the room. "I know."

She didn't say anything further. She wasn't sure there was anything *to* say. Addison simply stared out across the city. It was an overcast day, and she could see cars and people far below—each of them going about his or her day, most of them living ordinary, uncomplicated lives, while stories above, her world was falling apart.

William broke the silence. "Look, my security team is one of the best in the world. They wouldn't have brought you here if they thought you might be seen. This is what they do, Addison. They're experts."

She turned to him. "Being seen here—now—that's not what I'm worried about. What I'm worried about is done. And I can't take it back."

"I see."

She cocked her head. "If you have all of this… then why were you there that day… alone?"

"I broke the rules."

"Ah," she said. "Well, then we have at least one thing in common."

"I'd be willing to bet more."

She bit her lip. "Why?"

"Why?"

"Why did you break the rules that day?"

He shrugged. "I guess I just wanted to be a normal person… to see what it's like to be free of all of this."

She nodded slowly and then glanced back toward the window.

"But I don't regret it," he said catching her off guard.

She smiled wryly. "Not even on account of the time or the money?"

"Not one bit. I met you," he told her. "I just needed to bring you here to talk to you—to tell you in person how I feel. I wanted you to see that I'm a real person and I care about you."

"You don't even know me."

William stood and walked over to the window where she was standing. "Maybe not. But you haven't exactly given me a chance. I do know that what we had that day in the elevator was more than just sex. I know that I can't stop thinking about you. I know that every time I look at you, I'm surprised that I never want to stop. Tell me you don't feel it, Addison. Tell me you haven't thought of me, too."

"I—I don't know what you want me to say."

"I want you to tell me that I'm wrong. Just say the words and you can walk out of here and pretend this whole thing never happened."

As he spoke, Addison saw something in his eyes, something that she recognized. There was loneliness, a longing she knew all too well. But she saw something else, too: Sadness. Hunger. Passion. And that, she couldn't resist.

She swallowed. "I've never been that good at pretending."

"You see, then, we do have a few things in common after all," he said, his eyes focused intently on hers.

Right then and there, Addison planned all the ways in which she wanted to make that sadness go away. She hadn't planned on kissing him. But she did. And the rest, well, the rest came as a pleasant surprise.

CHAPTER NINE

Once she'd fed and bathed the boys and had finally gotten them off to bed, Addison sat down with a glass of wine and Sondra's envelope—anything to keep her mind off of what had transpired that afternoon. This time was different. This time she couldn't say it was a mistake. *Fool me once.* This time wasn't like the first time. She'd walked into that apartment willingly and this time she wasn't drunk. This time she remembered everything, every little detail.

Unable to keep the images from replaying over and over in her mind, she downed her glass, poured another, and tore into the envelope. The first page was a letter:

Dear Addison,

What I am about to propose will likely shock the hell out of you. Before you continue any further, I want you to promise to keep an open mind and give some careful consideration to what I am asking. If I didn't think that my proposition was a plausible solution to your situation, I would not be offering. I take what I am about to tell you very seriously and I hope you will, too. This is my life. This is my life's work.

In addition to my work at the agency, I own the most prestigious private dungeon in the state of Texas where I serve as Head Mistress. Mistress and Dominatrix are two words often intermixed with one another and are used to describe a dominant female who performs the art of domination and discipline as well as fantasy role-play. This profession is not illegal and to ease your mind upfront, I want to say that it has nothing to do with prostitution.

First of all, sex of any kind is prohibited, and the Mistresses I employ must be fully clothed at all times.

At this point you're probably wondering what any of this has to do with you. A good Dominatrix (or Mistress) is intelligent, articulate, quick-witted, creative, and good at improvisation—all qualities I see within you, Addison.

Professional Dominatrices take pride in their psychological insight into their client's "needs" and fetishes as well as their technical ability to perform complex BDSM practices, and other forms of bondage, suspension, torture role-play, and corporal punishment, as well as other such practices, which require a high degree of knowledge and competency to safely oversee.

Due to unforeseen medical complications, I would like to offer you the role as Head Mistress for a twelve-week term. During this period, in addition to your regular work and salary at The Carlisle Agency, you would be responsible for working ten hours maximum per week at a rate of

$15,000/week, completing sessions with my most exclusive clientele. At the end of the term, you will have earned $180,000. This is on top of your regular earnings.

There will be extensive training, which shall take place over the course of two weeks, beginning next Friday. During this training period and throughout the duration of your twelve-week term, you and your family will be provided with any and all staffing services The Carlisle Agency provides. This includes, but is not limited to round-the-clock car service, a personal chef, twenty-four-hour concierge, a personal assistant, live in nanny, and daily maid service.

Included in this envelope is a Mistress Handbook. Please read over the handbook and training materials before making your decision.

Again, I sincerely urge you to give this matter serious consideration, especially given your current situation. It's no secret that you are having an affair. What happens when the video tape is released? Can you properly support your children in the aftermath of a likely divorce, one in which you are the at-fault party?

That aside, I have no doubt that you are perfect for this role, Addison. In fact, I have handpicked you from a group of many, most of them already trained, highly experienced Domme's.

I look forward to discussing this with you further.

See you tomorrow at eight a.m. sharp.

Sincerely,
Sondra

What the fuck? She'd already taken her fair share of wrong turns, just that day alone, and now there was *this*. Sure, she'd consumed nearly a half a bottle of wine, but she certainly hadn't seen this one coming. *"Not a chance in hell,"* Addison told herself, as she lay tossing and turning, pondering her future and the freedom an additional $180,000 could give her.

~

THE FOLLOWING morning was gray and misty, the kind of day that nearly convinced one to pull the covers up and stay in bed. Addison considered for a moment calling in a mental health day. Mostly, she just needed to think. Perhaps tomorrow. Today she needed to talk with Sondra. Today she put this whole thing to bed and get back on track.

The boys had been excessively whiny and clingy since Patrick left—not that Addison hadn't expected as much. But expecting something doesn't make it any easier when it actually happens. With the thirteen-hour time difference between Beijing and Austin, neither she nor the kids had heard from Patrick all that much, and the distance was taking its toll. On one hand, she missed him. She missed having help around the house, even if it wasn't much. But it was the little things she missed most. The texts, the phone calls, the understanding that there was another person who had shared goals and interests, knowing that person was going to come home at the end of the day, and later in the dark, when you were most vulnerable, they'd curl their body into yours, letting you know where you belong

On the other hand, it didn't help that they'd never been

apart this long. Or that the longer he was away, the more angry and resentful she became. Addison's mind flip-flopped back and forth, from missing to hating him for choosing as he did, and this array of feelings was hard to reconcile.

ONCE ADDISON GOT the boys off to school, she headed into the office, her thoughts drifting to William. She had a full day ahead of her, which meant she had little time for distractions. Word about the agency seemed to be spreading, and they were busier than ever. Requests for placement were coming in so fast Sondra had said they would need to hire someone to help Addison within the next month or so.

Before heading to her boss's office, she checked herself in the mirror, barely recognizing the reflection staring back at her. Wearing a navy, sleek, wool crepe J Crew dress that had been impeccably tailored to fit, she looked elegant, sophisticated. Nothing like she felt on the inside and a far cry from the person she was just a few short months ago.

Addison took her phone from her bag and checked the screen. Three new emails, one of them from William. None from Patrick. She clicked on the email from William and noticed the butterflies flutter in her stomach. She hated herself for having them.

From: William B. Hartman

Date: 6/17/12

To: Addison Greyer

Subject: Grazie Per Ieri

Dearest Addison,

I can't seem to get you off of my mind.

I've thought of you a lot today. 817 times to be exact.

I need help.

Call me.

Baci Tutto,

William

Addison immediately opened up Google and typed *"Grazie Per Ieri* and *Baci Tutto."* Thank you for yesterday. And kisses all over. In Italian. Her heart skipped a beat. She smiled, unable to help herself.

From: Addison Greyer

Date: 6/17/12

To: William B. Hartman

Subject: English Translation

Dear Mr. Hartman,

You may not be aware of this, but I am not Italian.

And just so you know, in English, *Baci Tutto* translates as "time to put your guard up."

Sincerely,

Addison

P.S. 817 times? Don't you have a corporation to run?

She hit send and glanced at the clock. Seven fifty-nine a.m. *Shit.*

Hightailing it to Sondra's office, she knocked once before letting herself in.

Sondra didn't look up from her computer. "Morning, Mrs. Greyer."

Addison sat down in the chair across from Sondra's desk and folded her hands in her lap. She took a deep breath. *Better to get it over with.*

Sondra finally looked up, the look on her face offering nothing.

Addison sat up straighter. "I appreciate the offer, Sondra. I really do. But I'm sorry," she said. "I can't do it."

Sondra pressed her lips together. "I must say... I am disappointed, but not surprised."

Addison frowned, but said nothing. She knew the type of woman Sondra was and she knew she was going to let her have it. All she could do was wait it out. *Deny. Deny. Deny.*

What Sondra said next nearly knocked her over. "I'm not going to talk you into this. I am only going to say that you have a very bad habit of underestimating yourself. In turn, you allow everyone else to do the same. You let people walk all over you. Treat you however they like. So, they do. Addison, your marriage is crumbling. Your husband does what he pleases. He left the country with little regard to the effect that it would have on you, much less your children, and you stood by and watched it happen. So, like I said, I'm not going to talk you into it. But I would like to know one thing: when are you going to stop being a doormat and take charge of your life?"

Addison's mouth had gone dry. *What could she say?* That she was surprised that Sondra had such keen observation? That she had Addison pegged? It was one thing that she thought these things herself, that she knew it all deep down. But to hear someone else say it, to have someone who was practically a stranger verbalize these things out loud, shook her to her core.

"Aren't you going to tell me I'm mistaken?"

Addison didn't answer.

"Have I ever told you that I was once married, too?"

She shook her head. She wasn't surprised Sondra was divorced. She didn't seem like the kind of woman who was keen on compromise and it was hard to get far in any relationship without it. That is unless you're the boss.

Sondra continued, her voice low. "We were high-school sweethearts. We married young, straight out of college. He was the love of my life. Two years into our marriage, I came home one day to find him loading suitcases in his trunk. I thought maybe he had another business trip that maybe he'd forgotten to tell me about. But, no. He was leaving me, Addison. Turns out, he had fallen in love with his secretary. The funny thing, I hadn't a clue that he was having an affair. A few weeks after he left, I found myself staring at two lines on a pregnancy test. We were going to have a baby, but he wasn't coming back. Said he had moved on with his life and that I should, too. I was in shock. Devastated. Four weeks later, I moved my stuff into a tiny apartment because it was all I was going to be able to afford with a baby as a single mother. As I sat in that tiny apartment, surveying my new life, finally feeling hopeful, I began bleeding profusely. In the ambulance on the way to the hospital, I nearly bled out. *I almost died.* I didn't. But there was a part of me that was never the same. I lost the baby and was told that I'd never be able to have children. While I lay there in that hospital bed for three weeks recovering, he never visited or even called. Not once."

"I'm sorry, Sondra," Addison said, hot tears stinging her cheeks. She hadn't meant to cry. But she was tired. And everything was catching up with her.

"Don't be. I learned a valuable lesson then, you see. I learned I was never going to put myself in that position again. I'm telling you all of this because I see a little bit of myself in you. I ended up broke, alone, and scared. I don't want to see what happened to me happen to you."

Addison stared at her hands. "I am . . . *We* are fine."

"Just think about it a little more, ok? Give it a few days."

Addison stood to go.

"Ok," she said, in the end. This time without looking back.

CHAPTER TEN

S ondra Sheehan was the sort of woman who didn't take no for an answer. Being petite, she learned early in life that she'd have to make up what she lacked in size with straight-up bravado. With a short red bob and deep green eyes, Sondra was elegant and a little unpleasant. Always well put together, not a single hair out of place, she liked order and carried herself in a way that let everyone know the high standards she'd set for them without her ever having to utter the words. Yet, for someone always in control, she found herself completely taken aback by her current predicament.

Addison Greyer had to take her up on her offer. She just had to. There was just no way around it. Time was running out for Sondra. She realized she'd have to make a decision soon. Having Addison fill in for her as Head Mistress was a brilliant idea, one that had come to Sondra almost completely by accident. Sure, Sondra had a lengthy list of women that she could have chosen for the role, but she wanted Addison. You see, Sondra was smart, extremely savvy, and knew deep down that none of these women quite fit the bill. Not like Addison did. First of all, she didn't trust any of them to handle her business and her clients in the same manner that she would. But mostly, it was the fact that Sondra didn't trust that they wouldn't steal her business right out from under her. These women were ruthless, which was, for the most part, a necessity in the business they were in. On the other hand, Sondra understood that this also disqualified them from being true leaders. A leader needed to be firm, but vulnerable. Smart, but willing to learn. Assertive, yet open.

Though she would never let on, from the moment she met Addison, Sondra liked her, which was a rare thing because Sondra liked very few people. There was something about Addison, though. Something different. For one, Sondra saw her as an underdog: The least likely to win, yes, but also as someone who had a fighting spirit. If one only looked hard enough, it was there. She knew that, like herself with the right mentor, Addison could become a winner.

The situation in the elevator only added to the mystery. Admittedly, without this piece of the puzzle, Sondra never would've considered taking on such a daunting task in her current state. Getting Mrs. Greyer into fighting shape was really more than she wanted to take on, and had she not found out about Addison's impromptu affair with William Hartman, she never would've considered it.

But as fate would have it, it was her star client who'd informed her of the videotape. A high-profile attorney, thrilled, yet shameful about selling it, he brought the information to her in a session. It was easy putting two and two together once Mr. Hartman called her about hiring Addison. If Sondra hadn't known better, she'd have thought it a purely brilliant maneuver for Mrs. Greyer to land herself a job this way. As a matter of fact, she was disappointed when she learned this wasn't exactly how it'd all played out.

While it didn't exactly surprise her that Addison hadn't

said yes to her offer right away, she was perplexed as to how to make her see the light. She'd dangled a carrot in front of her with the money and the help. She thought she'd drove the nail in the coffin when she mentioned the divorce and what it would do to her. But no. Addison didn't seem to be swayed by money or hardship. Of course, there was the other thing, too. The bigger thing. She hadn't asked about Sondra's medical condition and the reason Sondra needed to step out. Any of these things alone would have been enough. But all of them together only reaffirmed what Sondra knew to be true: Mrs. Greyer was perfect for the role. Money wasn't her main motivation. She respected privacy, yet she had an openness about her that made you want to tell her the truth. Any Mistress, especially Head Mistress, had to have this quality, and it was a rarity. It was upon this realization that Sondra realized what she had to do to get Addison to accept the offer. Then and there, she'd decided it was time to tell her the truth.

ADDISON'S DAY was filled with wall-to-wall meetings, which she was grateful for because it kept her mind focused on work and off of the shit storm that seemed to be surrounding her at the moment.

Penny, her mother-in-law, had been breathing down her neck ever since Patrick had announced he was taking the promotion. She'd already called three times this morning, and Penny was the last thing Addison either needed or wanted to deal with right then.

Thankfully, her first two meetings had been successful. She'd closed both deals and was on her way to close the third when Patrick called.

"Hello."

"Hey there. How are you?" Patrick asked, sounding upbeat.

"I'm good—just running between meetings. How are you?"

Addison checked her watch, calculating what time it had to be now in China.

"Tired. But good. Things are going better than expected. Listen, this is really premature, but there has been some talk about extending the project, and I was wondering what you'd think about living here—in China."

Addison pinched the bridge of her nose. The shit storm didn't seem to be letting up any time soon. "I don't know, Patrick."

Silence.

"Well, give it some thought, ok? Give the boys a hug and tell them I miss them."

"Will do," she said flatly.

She heard something falter, a change in his breathing. He was tired. "Addison, I miss you. I know you're angry, but it doesn't have to be this way, you know."

She stared at the clear blue sky, contemplating what to say.

"I know," Addison finally muttered, realizing it was all she could offer.

~

ADDISON CLOSED on the third deal and headed back to the office to quickly wrap things up for the day before it was time to pick up the boys. Opening up her email to send a few contracts, she smiled.

From: William B. Hartman

Date: 6/18/12

To: Addison Greyer

Subject: Speaking in Italian

Dear Mrs. Greyer,

Never underestimate the investigative tools at my disposal. I am fully aware that you are not Italian. It could be the blonde hair, blue eyes and the fairest skin my lips have ever touched. But who's to say? :)

That said, I was testing the waters to see if you may enjoy speaking Italian.

I have to travel to Capri on business, and I want you to come with me. Bring the boys if you'd like. They'll love it.

I've arranged it with your boss.

We leave in two days.

Il Vostro,

William

P.S. I can't wait to see the beaches of Capri reflected in your eyes.

Seriously. *I've made arrangements with your boss.* Who does he think he is? Addison stood and paced the length of her office. Certainly, he didn't think it was just that easy. For one, she didn't even know him. Two, she couldn't just jet off to Italy. She had responsibilities. But that's not what pissed her off most. What bothered her more was how much she wished she could—how badly she *wanted* to go. Addison grabbed her purse and headed out, first calling her mother-in-law to ask her to pick up the boys. She hated to do it, knowing and dreading the trouble it would bring. But she needed to clear her mind. She needed to see William.

PENNY GREYER RECEIVED the call to pick up her grandsons without a second to spare, which was, of course, exactly the kind of thing her daughter-in-law would pull. Addison liked putting her on the spot; she enjoyed making her jump through hoops. Thank goodness Penny had Rosie, or God knows what she would've done. Penny knew it was just a matter of time after her son left that Addison would crumble. There was no way a girl of her means could survive alone, not the way Penny had all those years. Her daughter-in-law didn't have what it takes to put her husband or her children first—which is why she had tried everything in her power to dissuade Patrick from marrying that girl in the first place. She begged him to quit seeing her, she knew Addison's type immediately. She wanted what all women want: security. But she wanted Patrick for more than just security. She wanted him for his family's money and Penny would be damned if some cute little gold-digger was getting one red cent of it. She told her son that from the get-go, even going so far as to offer him a bit of inheritance early if he'd stop seeing her and then when that didn't work, she'd cut him off completely. But it didn't last. Of course, it didn't. Her husband saw to that. You can't help who you love, he'd said. So, Penny tried setting him up with a few girls more like her, but it was futile. Addison had already sank her teeth into him She had some sort of hold on him that Penny couldn't and wouldn't ever understand. Besides the fact that Addison had given Penny beautiful grandbabies, although thankfully they got most of their looks and smarts from their father's side, there was nothing blatantly obvious that Penny could see that was especially wonderful about her. She was merely average—certainly, nothing special. What Patrick saw in her, she'd yet to figure out.

Truth be told, that's why he took the position so far away. He couldn't take admitting that he'd been wrong about his wife. Better to use distance as an excuse for a failed marriage rather than come to terms with the fact that he'd just plain chosen poorly.

But he missed his children; he loved them so. She knew this because, although he'd never said it directly, he called her and told her he was worried. While he made her promise to be nice to his wife, he had called her nonetheless, asking her to check on the kids. Penny had certainly tried, that was for sure. Of course, their mother enjoyed keeping her away from her grandchildren. That's the kind of person she was. So, as you can imagine, it shocked Penny when Addison called her asking for a favor. Really threw her for a loop. And this was how she knew that Addison was up to something. Penny even told her husband as much. He might've thought she was crazy. But she'd show him. And her son, too.

Her husband asked her not to meddle. For goodness sakes Penny, just let them be. But she couldn't.

"We know Patrick took that promotion in China just to get away from her, to get as far away as he could," she'd said.

"Maybe he just wanted the job, dear. Had you thought of that?"

"But he misses his children, Clark."

"Who wouldn't?"

"No, it's more than that. He called me, worried, asking me to check in on them. It's just a matter of time before she loses it. I'm telling you. I just know it," Penny told him, throwing up her hands. She paced. "She doesn't have what it takes. You know she's not good enough for him. And she's certainly not good enough to raise those precious babies. Clark, we've got to do something."

He shook his head slowly. "What is it that you want to do, Penny?"

She smiled. Finally, he was listening. "I'm not sure yet. But I'm thinking on it. Trust me."

Penny thought long and hard about what her husband had said. He thought she needed a plan and he was right. She would do something, anything, and quick. That woman was a terrible example for her precious, innocent grandchildren. At least her son had a choice in the matter. Her poor grandchildren never did. But that was about to change. It had to. Her daughter-in-law was up to something, and knowing her, it was no good. Penny was determined to find out what that something was. No one divided her family and got away with it. In the end, she'd show her.

CHAPTER ELEVEN

Addison had given it a lot of thought. This had to stop. The e-mails, phone calls, the off-the-wall sex, and invitations to Italy... they all needed to stop. She would tell William whatever it was they were doing, it had to end. Everything. All of it. *Game over.*

Sure, she was sad and lonely, and sure, William Hartman was dark, fun, and exciting, but she was a wife and a mother and what she was doing was wrong. There was simply no way around it, no justification that could make what she was doing ok, even in her own mind, especially *not* in her own mind. Addison knew she had to get a hold on the situation before it was too late.

She dug her phone out of her purse and texted William.

I need to see you.

He replied a few seconds later: **The feeling is mutual. I'm in my office. Top floor. Where are you?**

Addison felt her face grow hot and her pulse quicken. She hadn't exactly put two and two together before now, that all she had to do if she wanted to see him was to take the elevator a few floors up, realizing he worked in the same building. *His building.*

Addison: **Leaving my office now.**

William: **Come up. My receptionist will see you in.**

Addison thought twice about going, knowing it was risky. *Maybe not everything needed to be said.* But after weighing her options, she decided she needed to look him in the eye when she said it. Also, it was probably less risky than meeting him anywhere else. Not to mention, since she was calling things off, she knew he couldn't cause a scene at the office, and there was little to no risk of her sleeping with him there.

William's beautiful, but disapproving, secretary showed Addison in. She wasn't exactly rude, but Addison knew the look well. She kept her back straight and her head high.

If she'd learned anything in the past few weeks, it was that you have to look and own the part, even when you don't feel like it. Her clients and potential clients were some of the wealthiest men and women in the world. They smelled bullshit a mile away. So that's exactly what she'd intended to do walking into William's office that day: play the part.

Addison had to admit, she was a bit surprised walking into William's office. Of course, it was gorgeous but it was something more. There was something about the way he sat behind his desk legs up, feet crossed, chewing on his pen, staring at her intently. He was in his element, more himself than she'd seen him before. He owned the space, and of course, that made him all the more attractive.

"So, you *needed* to see me," William said, his voice deep and sultry, lingering on the word needed a few seconds too long.

So, he'd decided to play a part, too.

Addison sat down in the chair opposite his desk and crossed her legs. *Keep it professional. Easy in. Easy out.*

"I needed to speak with you, actually," she said looking

away and then back at him. "I figured it was best in person...I
... Uh . . . We . . ." she started and then paused in order to
find the words she needed. "This has to stop, William... I'm
married to a wonderful man, and we have three children.
While I appreciate your offer, I think we both know that this
is wrong," she told him with a heavy sigh. "I'm sorry that I let
it go on this long."

William didn't bat an eye. He leaned back in his chair,
glaring at her. "Are you *really*, though?"

"Am I really though *what*?"

"Sorry," he said. "Are you really married to a wonderful
man? Because I'm not buying it."

"I beg your pardon?" Addison asked, raising her voice
slightly. "Of course, I am."

William looked around the office and then met her gaze
head on. "And just where is this wonderful man you're
married to?"

"Working."

He stood and walked to the other side of the desk where
she sat. "Working," he repeated. "Well, that's one way to look
at it."

She shook her head. "That's the only way."

William scoffed. "He left you, Addison. He left you *here* to
deal with everything. He chose a promotion over his family.
Over you."

Addison balled her fists, certain that if she'd been
standing she would've slapped him.

She stood to leave. *Keep it together.* "Like I said, this is over.
As for my private life, I'm not sure what business it is of
yours."

William grabbed her chin, forcing her to look at him.
"You made it my business. I know you don't mean what
you're saying. You're smarter than that. Maybe you can buy
your own bullshit, but don't expect me to."

She needed to go before she lost all resolve, before her knees buckled beneath her. "I'm not lying," she told him. "I can't do this."

"Suit yourself." William leaned toward her, kissing her ever so gently at the corner of her mouth, not a full on kiss, but not exactly an innocent kiss on the cheek, either. Addison put her hand to her face, feeling the buzz where his lips had just been. *This man knows what he's doing. Leave. Now.*

She started to go but he grabbed her hand, intertwining their fingers. He lifted her chin, raising her gaze to meet his. "Just in case no one's told you—it's ok to be a little bit selfish every now and then. If you want to go, go. But, if you want to stay, I promise to do everything in my power to make you happy. I know this isn't easy. And I understand you have a lot at stake, but I promise to protect you as best I can."

Addison exhaled slowly and then leaned forward resting her head on his chin. She felt his lips slowly trailing south and she knew she couldn't stop it, even if she'd wanted to. *It's ok to be a little selfish every now and then.* Soon, they were entangled in a heap on the floor, making love as though nothing else mattered and they'd never be asked to pay for their mistakes.

When they were finished, they lay there staring at each other for a long while before William broke the silence by whispering in her ear. "It'll be the death of me if our meetings keep ending like this."

She laughed. "I'm certain of it."

"Come to Italy with me. Please. I want you there."

"You know I can't...."

William kissed the tip of her ear. "Why not? We'll have separate rooms. I worked it out with Sondra. You can bring the boys. I don't see the problem."

"You wouldn't," she said, distracted.

Addison sat up. "How do you know Sondra anyway? And how do you know *so* much about me?"

"It's my job. It's what I do. Research."

"You mean take-overs?"

He grinned. "I like to think of it more in terms of mergers."

There on the floor of William's office, with those words uttered, the matter was settled. Addison had always wanted to visit Italy. Mistake or no mistake, she decided she'd be crazy not to jump at the chance when it presented itself.

LATER THAT EVENING, when Addison picked up the boys from her in-laws, she explained that she had to go out of town on business to handle a client situation and asked Penny if she'd mind checking in on the kids for a few days. Addison had already decided that it was best if they stayed with their nanny, Kelsey, whom they adored, in their own home. While it was kind of William to offer to bring them along, Addison never once considered that an option.

Still, she knew making the offer to Penny would complicate things. For one, she'd have to explain the trip to her in-laws *and* her husband. But she knew how much Penny wanted to be included and in the end, Addison wanted to do the right thing, especially given how much of the wrong things she'd been doing lately. Thankfully, to her surprise, Penny was supportive of the trip and her idea, which Addison saw as a positive sign since her mother-in-law had never once been supportive of anything she did. Finally, it seemed things were making a turn for the better.

Two days later, Addison and William boarded a private jet headed for Naples, Italy. Addison saw the trip as a break, as time to think. She had a lot on her mind, knowing she needed to make a decision in regards to Sondra's offer as well as Patrick's suggestion that she and the boys move to China. She figured getting away from the day in and day out of it all would give her a better perspective.

Patrick hadn't been thrilled with her impromptu trip to Italy and urged her to quit her job when she said she had to go. It was taking too much time away from where she needed to focus her attention: on her children and their home, he'd said. *If he only knew . . .*

Italy was nothing short of amazing. From the sights to the smells, and the food to the language, Addison was fascinated. Upon arrival in Naples, they were driven by Carl and several members of William's security team to a ferry that would take them to the isle of Capri where a boat was waiting to take them to their final destination: a private villa that belonged to one of William's business associates. The whole thing was so carefully orchestrated it concerned Addison. William seemed to take it all in stride, but for her, this was a vastly different way of living. Having someone tell you where to be, and when to be there, not to mention having so many resources at your disposal was a foreign concept to her. Almost as foreign as the destination itself.

"Why do you wear a suit every day if you're on vacation?" Addison asked one morning.

"This isn't vacation. This is business."

Addison cocked her head. "How do you separate the two?"

He walked to the bed where she was sitting and stood

over her. "Very, very poorly."

$\sim$

WILLIAM HAD KEPT HIS WORD. They had separate bedroom suites, though she found that he seemed to spend most of his time in hers. William, it turned out, was fun to be around, even when they weren't in the sack. He was serious when he needed to be and entertaining when he didn't.

"Are you glad you came?" he asked one afternoon catching her off guard. She'd been working on her laptop in his bed. He'd been reading on the couch adjacent.

"Yes," she told him, honestly.

"Come here," he replied. "I want to ask your opinion on something..."

Addison did as he'd asked. He showed her several documents from a deal he said he was working on. She scanned through them unsure of what he wanted from her. "Well?"

"What?" she asked looking up.

"What do you think?"

Addison furrowed her brow. "It's your business... not mine..."

"I want to know what you think..."

She shrugged. "It doesn't matter what I think."

"Of course it matters. Otherwise I wouldn't have asked."

Addison bit her lip and gave it some thought. "I don't think you should sign..."

"Why not?"

"I don't know. I just don't."

"I think you do know."

"Fine," she relented. "Because if you really wanted to do it, you wouldn't be asking my opinion. That means you aren't sure."

He smiled. "We could stay here awhile, you know."

Addison looked away. "No," she said. "We can't."

"Well," he countered, standing. "I'm glad one of us is sure of something."

~

WILLIAM HARTMAN WAS the happiest that he'd been in perhaps, well, in forever really. He was here on the beautiful isle of Capri where he was about to close a major deal, an acquisition that he'd been working on for years. It wasn't only that the deal was going to close and he could finally put it behind him or that it would make him an extreme amount of money that had put him in such a good mood. It was the fact that he was here with the first girl he'd ever cared to get to know.

There had been many women in and out of his life but none he'd wanted to keep around. The problem he found with these women was that they were addicted to and in love with his lifestyle, not so much with him. He'd first witnessed this with his own mother who was always looking for a way to advance up the food chain, yet with each marriage, finding herself more and more miserable. William was determined not to make the same mistakes she did. So, he threw himself into his work and didn't look back. It's not exactly like he was lonely, there always seemed to be a ready replacement for the last disaster who'd occupied his bed. But he had a rule. Two weeks max. That's how long he kept them around. Not a day longer. Most didn't last that long as it was. That was the thing about William. He didn't like most people. He didn't care for idle chitchat and he didn't want to have to concern himself with another person's emotional needs. He was bad at emotions, even he knew that. The longer he kept them around the more they grated on his nerves. With each passing day, the needier they became.

The thing that William found most unsettling was that the more he pulled away, the tighter the women clung on, each one trying harder than the last to prove that she could be whatever she thought it was he was looking for. And when that didn't work, they would assure him they were willing and able to put up with his philandering ways. What they didn't understand was what they were buying into was a myth. He didn't want a woman who devalued and disrespected herself, who was willing to put up with being treated in a way that was less than she deserved. He wanted standards.

On the other end of the spectrum were the businesswomen he bedded: powerful women looking to prove that they didn't *need* any man, only to reveal in their next breath that they were looking to take over the world and would appreciate using his knowledge and assets to do so. That was always the kicker about the ones with standards. They'd trample right over him if it meant winning.

"You're different," he told her over lunch.

"Me?"

William glanced around the room. "Who else?"

Addison stuffed a bite into her mouth, savoring it. "This is so good..."

"I've never met anyone like you."

"You have to try that tomato," she said. She pointed her fork at his plate. "Seriously, try it." Her eyes lit up.

"You seem oblivious to the way people look at you."

Addison inhaled. "Oh, my God. Have you tasted—"

"Goddamnit. I don't give a fuck about the food, Addison," William said, harshly. He laid his palm flat on the table, his eyes boring into hers. "I'm sorry."

Addison pressed her lips together and raised her brow. "What *do* you give a fuck about?"

He seemed to think long and hard about her question, about how to answer it. "Look—" he said eventually. "I know you have children. And quite frankly, that scares the shit out of me."

Addison cut in. "What do my kids have to do with any of this?"

"Are you kidding? They have everything to do with this."

She swallowed hard and he knew he'd touched the core of who she was. He also knew that was no simple matter. Addison wasn't the kind of woman who let you near her core all that often. She kept it guarded, protected, tucked away. They had that much in common. He watched her shift, watched a veil come down. "I don't know what you want me to say," she told him, matter of factly.

"I'm not ready for this to end."

She smiled. "Oh," she said, her eyes challenging him. "It's just getting started."

"Is that so?"

"Yes—and if you'll let me finish my lunch and you know... actually eat your own... I'll show you."

SHE DID SHOW HIM. He'd wanted to finish the conversation, to say what he needed to say, but she'd have none of it.

"I just want you to know," he told her after they'd made love, windows open, the sound of the ocean in the background, the breeze the only witness to their pleasure. "I understand that children aren't pawns; they aren't something to take for granted."

"Good to know," she said, tracing lines across his chest.

"Don't you want to discuss this...?"

Addison shook her head. "What's there to discuss? We're just having fun."

"Oh," he said smugly. "Is that what this is?"

He felt her smile against his chest. "*I* think so."

~

ADDISON DRIFTED off into a post lunch/post sex nap. He watched her sleep noticing that the expression on her face was only stated. He knew that look. And he thought he knew the reason for it. This thing they had going, it wouldn't last. Not because she didn't want it to, but because she couldn't let it.

He'd wanted to tell her that he thought he could love her. He'd wanted to say that he would take care of her. He certainly had the means. But he didn't say any of that, not in the end. He was too busy thinking about something else: fatherhood. The truth was, he hadn't given it much thought before then, but lying there with her, something shifted within him, a switch was flipped and he began to worry about something in a way that he'd never worried about before: whether or not he'd be a good father. William excelled at everything he tried; he didn't want fatherhood to be the one thing he messed up. It was hard to say, seeing that he himself had never had a father, and since his own mother didn't have a maternal bone in her body, he worried that maybe it was genetic. She saw William as her meal ticket, and she took it, leaving the rest up to the slew of nannies she employed.

The fact that Addison was married hadn't bothered him at first. He'd dated his fair share of married women and had never really given it much thought, until he met this married woman and she hadn't returned his calls and emails or responded to the flowers he sent.

William was all the more confounded when she seemed determined to put their affair behind her and focus on her marriage. This just didn't happen to him. Rejection was a new concept. Things came easy for William. Everything except love. Real love. So, when he saw it written upon Addison's face as she spoke of her husband and children, when he felt her restraint and knew she was holding back, when most women would've given in, that was it for him.

He wanted that. He wanted her. He knew that he would do everything within his power to win. Lucky for him, this was his sweet spot. After all, takeovers and acquisitions were his specialty.

DESPITE TRYING to keep her distance, Addison was falling for William. It would've been hard for any woman not to, but for someone in her situation it was damn near impossible. Addison needed to know she mattered. Particularly since Patrick had made the decision he had and William was extremely charming, he did everything he could to see that she was comfortable and happy. But there was more to him than meets the eye, she realized that. He was the kind of man that needed saving. She surprised herself that when he'd asked about her upbringing, she'd told him. That was the beauty of having an affair, she'd decided. You could be completely yourself, because there wasn't time for anything else. It wasn't going to last.

IF IT WAS GOING to hurt, and it was, Addison figured why hold back. That's why she made the life-altering decision to accept Sondra's offer.

Lying on a chaise lounge by the pool, overlooking the expanse of the ocean with her head on William's chest and the warm sun shining upon her face, she decided she'd do it. She couldn't put her finger on it, couldn't nail down the exact reason why in her mind, only that she felt it was the right choice to make. It was more of a hunch, really. A feeling that something was about to change and that taking the role and ultimately the money was the smart thing to do. She didn't need to ask anyone. *She was sure.*

What she hadn't decided was whether or not she and the boys would move to China and reunite with Patrick. What she did know was, that no matter how welcome the distraction or how well it soothed her hurt, no matter how amazing the sex or how beautiful the location, her heart wasn't completely there. It was at home with her children, her life. And part of it was in China with Patrick. Sure, they had their share of problems and had certainly made mistakes, but that didn't erase their history. It didn't erase the years, the decade of marriage, or all of the good times they'd shared.

That was the thing about marriage. It's never all good or all bad. It's just two people doing the best they can. Addison's mind flashed back to memories of Patrick with Connor as a baby, and then to him cheering as the twins were delivered. She pictured him on their wedding day, and she realized what she already knew, that she missed him, that she loved him, and that she wanted to be a family.

But, whether or not she was willing to uproot everyone and leave a job she loved to do so, was another matter altogether. She'd have to give it a lot of thought. And later, once William left to attend a series of meetings, she decided she'd sit by the pool and pore over the training materials Sondra had given her. In hindsight, she would come to understand that sometimes not choosing was in actuality doing just that.

CHAPTER TWELVE

Addison awoke in William's arms as he lowered her gently down onto the bed.

"What time is it?" she asked, yawning, forcing her eyes open.

"Two o'clock. You fell asleep by the pool. I didn't want to wake you..."

She rubbed her eyes, confused. "Why'd you let me sleep that long?"

William smiled. "Why not?"

Addison took hold of his shirt and pulled him down on the bed toward her, kissing him lightly on his lips. She knew her time there with him was limited. She didn't want to waste a second of it. *What was it about this man that drove her to the edge?*

She picked up her pace, lifting his shirt over his head. His body was now a deep shade of brown. *So, this is what he looks like tan.* She hadn't thought it possible for him to look any better than he had that first time. But he did. "Addison, I can't. I have to go. My meeting is in half an hour."

She grazed the edge of his jaw with her tongue. "This won't take that long. Promise."

William laughed, though his gaze was serious, focused. "No, really, Addison. I have to go," he replied, gently removing her from his lap, placing her on the bed.

She scoffed. "Oh, and here I was assuming you were the boss."

William leaned in, kissing her firmly. He lingered. "Wow. That was a low blow. But you know . . . you're pretty cute when you pout."

Addison rolled her eyes and plopped herself playfully backward on the bed, sighing loudly.

William scooped her up. "That's it—you asked for it."

He carried her to the bathroom and placed her on the counter, took his cell phone from his pocket and shot off a text. Then he slipped out of his bathing suit. "Well. What do you fancy? Here? Or in the shower?"

Addison grinned. "How about both."

LATER, after he'd dressed and gone, Addison threw on her swimsuit, gathered her training materials and made her way back down to the pool. Glancing behind her, she saw a man she'd heard William refer to as Joe following not far behind. He was on William's security team and never seemed to be too far behind any time she left her room. This time, just as before, she did her best to pretend he wasn't there.

The first day after they'd arrived at the villa she questioned William about why *she* needed security when he was the likely target. He spoke in a clipped tone, only saying that if she were to be traveling with him then she required the same level of protection. *Protection from what,* she'd asked. *Let it be,* he'd said, and noticing the way his demeanor changed and his jaw tightened, she did.

ADDISON SAT DOWN and flipped through her booklet before opening it, trying to ensure that Joe didn't get too close. *They'll keep their distance, William had said.*

She turned the first page:

Lessons for a Dominatrix.

LESSON #1: (THIS IS MOST IMPORTANT OF ALL!):
Being a Dominant is 99% mental.

You must believe in and harness your power or you cannot expect anyone else to. This takes a lot of preparation and training. But it is the first and foremost important rule of being a Mistress. You are playing a role, much like an actress plays a role. A Mistress must nail her part each and every time. She must tune in to what her audience needs from her and fulfill those needs. Leave them wanting more. Always remember, you become brave by acting brave.

LESSON #2: Sessions provide an experience.

Potential submissives (slaves) often ask what is involved in a BDSM session. They want to know what services are involved. The very use of that word "service" shows that the majority of people still see BDSM as some sort of service to be provided, akin to a massage, a haircut, or a visit to a brothel. Perhaps there are some Mistresses that place them-selves in that category of "service provider." Not at Dungeon Seven. Money, often referred to as a tribute, never exchanges hands between Mistress and sub. All tributes are handled prior to the session, taking place by a third party, the receptionist at Seven. When one wishes to have a session with one of our Mistresses, he is informed of how We at Seven approach the concept of a session.

First, our Mistresses do not provide services. It is the submissive (sub or slave) that makes him/herself available to serve the Mistress. It's better to think of a session as a lesson. When coming for a session, a submissive expects to be taken on a journey: an inner journey into the realms of the mind, into one's intimate senses. A session is an experience. Now, how much one gains from a session depends on his ability to learn, surrender, and trust his Mistress. While previous experience is not a requirement, only an eagerness to go on the journey, the clients at Seven are properly vetted and undergo an extensive selection process.

LESSON #3: You will see the same rotation of six clients during the duration of your term as Head Mistress. Never anyone else.

Included in your training materials, I have provided lengthy, detailed information on each client you will see. You will study their likes and dislikes, as well as specific information about what happens in an average session with that particular client. Explicit detail about each client's specific and individual needs and deepest desires should be learned both forward and backward.

A good sub (slave) remembers all rules set up by his owner. He will do his best to uphold those rules and keep within the set boundaries. Keep in mind, some subs like to push their Mistress, challenge her authority or be naughty; this only works if the Domme is compliant in such games. If not, the sub is breaking the golden rule by putting his own needs above his Mistress's. This behavior must not be tolerated.

Commit this information to memory, as you will be tested. Remember, the submissives I am entrusting you with are my *most* valuable clients, and they must be treated with the utmost respect and care.

LESSON #4: Rules of a Session. Subs understand them. YOU enforce them.

A session begins with the submissive undressing and sitting in the chair in the middle of the room. The Mistress then fastens a black leather collar around the sub's neck, which marks the beginning of the session.
The sub must always ask permission before he/she says or does anything. **PERIOD**!

A sub must always use the proper form of address when speaking to you. They must ask, "Mistress, may I have permission to speak?"

Submissives are never to say, "No," when their Mistress instructs them to do something. If they don't follow the rules of the session, it is imperative that they are disciplined.

The "Safe Word" is "**MERCY.**" Subs know to use this word when the situation becomes unbearable. Do not take this lightly. Stop the session and talk it out. Tune in to body language; use your intuition to determine when more or less is required within a session. Remember, each session is different and treat it as such.

LESSON 5: Never underestimate your role as Mistress. Respect it. Uphold yourself to the highest standard at all times. Expect the same from your subs.

As Mistress, you are considered a therapist of sorts. Being a sub can take on many forms: being a slave, being told what to do, crawling around on all fours at Mistress's feet, being kept on a leash or chain, feeding from a bowl, various fetishes, role playing, and, of course, being punished when naughty and rewarded when compliant. All of these scenarios stem from the same desire: the willing and joyful surrender of control. For a sub, nothing can be more liberating than this— to step out of the "real world," relinquish responsibility, worries, and everyday pressures, and hand over his life to another.

Being a submissive is not a one-way exchange. It's not about being helpless, being a victim, being lazy, and expecting someone else to do everything for you; it's the eagerness to serve, to worship another, the willingness and desire to please. Submission is a ritualized role of surrender and devotion to another. And if there's one golden rule that reigns above all others in being a proper sub, it is "THE DESIRE TO SERVE."

It is essential that you understand the psychology involved in being a Mistress, the psychology behind what we do at Seven. My clients consist of high-ranking members of society: CEOs, physicians, attorneys, and wonderfully brilliant men from all over the business spectrum. What they have in common is that they come to Seven to create an environment where they don't need to think, where they don't have to be "on" and in charge and in control.

These clients are looking for an escape, the chance to let go. So, they come to a place where they can trust me as Mistress to keep them safe while I weave together an enticing, thrilling, euphoric, and painful world where it is literally impossible to think. For some of them, it simply boils down to the fact that they do not have the freedom to explore their fantasies, desires, or sexuality with their partners.

You must understand that the majority of my clients experience an extreme imbalance of power in their lives. For some, it stems from extreme disempowerment, like child abuse, neglect, or poverty; for others, it is an overwhelming burden of power, related to everything from wealth to politics.

Addison closed the booklet and stared out at the ocean, suddenly feeling exhausted. *What was she thinking? Who was she kidding, thinking she could handle this?* She'd finish reading the training material and the client profiles, mostly because she was curious, but once she arrived back home, she realized she had to face Sondra and tell her that she just couldn't do it. Only it wasn't for the reasons one might think. Addison found herself consumed by the rush, the range of emotions evoked and the thrill she got when she imagined what saying yes would look like. Overwhelmed by the mixture of fear and excitement coursing through her veins, her imagination led her to dark places in her mind. Places she wasn't ready to admit existed.

WILLIAM RETURNED to find Addison down by the water. He stayed back, watching her. He watched the way she stared at the ocean, the facial expressions she made as she ran the sand between her hands. *God, she was beautiful. This one was going to*

be different. This one was going to be hard to let go. He sat, thinking that he could stay here forever with her and be perfectly happy. Tomorrow they were scheduled to head home, where she would go back to her family and he would go back to the work that consumed him.

It bothered William that he felt so restless. It wasn't a feeling he was used to having. Not only that, but he had just closed on one of the largest acquisitions of his career, so why in the world did he feel so low? *That's what love feels like. The highs are like nothin' else... but man, those lows.*

Addison spotted him sitting there. Something crossed her face, surprise maybe. She smiled and ran toward him. Pouncing, she knocked him backward. He allowed himself to be taken down. Lifting his hands above his head, she pinned them there. "You're back," she said, tickling him. William squirmed. She frowned, noticing his dark suit. "But not exactly dressed for the occasion."

William raised his eyebrows and shrugged. She began tugging on his tie, unbuttoning his shirt. "Well," she said. "That's a pity. One in which we'll have to change." He looked on as she untied his shoes and removed them without taking her eyes from his. She removed his socks and pants, leaving him in his boxers. He eyed her intently, studying her, from the way she licked her lips unknowingly, to the little expressions she made.

Addison climbed on top of him; placing her hands on both sides of his face, she searched his eyes. "Why so serious?"

William smirked. "No reason."

She sat back, crossing her arms. "Hmm... I'm not buying it," she said, before running her hand through the sand. Eventually, she looked towards the horizon. "Someone wise once uttered those words to me, anyway."

"I'm in love with you, Addison."

She froze. Her whole body, it just seized up. "Please don't say that. You hardly know me."

"I know enough."

She stood, dusting herself off and reached for his hand. "Come in the water with me."

William pushed himself up, scooped Addison off the ground by her knees and threw her over his shoulder. "So, you think I'm too serious, huh?"

"Put me down," she begged as William waded further out into the water. Once the water reached his knees, William set her down. She surprised him by hugging his neck as she hung on, squeezing his waist with her thighs.

"You're certainly not helping matters any, you know," William told her, noting the way their bodies fit perfectly together. "Oh, by the way, I accepted an invitation for a last-minute business lunch tomorrow, right before we leave. I want you to come with me."

Her eyes narrowed and she chewed on her bottom lip, taking it between her teeth. "That's probably not such a good idea."

"Says who?"

She leaned forward then and kissed his neck, tasting the salt on his skin. Noticing the way the muscles in his chest flexed against her tongue, she moved lower. "If I didn't know better, Mrs. Greyer, I'd say you were trying to distract me."

"Never," she whispered against his skin, biting just a little.

"I think, maybe, I'm in over my head," William murmured.

"Not yet," Addison had said right before he made love to her there in the water, both of them fully aware they were being watched. When they were finished, they stayed that way, tangled and floating together, riding the waves for a little while. Neither of them wanting to come back to shore. Neither of them wanting to face reality.

CHAPTER THIRTEEN

Patrick Greyer hated China from day one. Despised it. Why he'd even agreed to move there, he had no idea. It was a mistake. He should be back in Texas where he belonged with his family and the woman he loved. The woman he *really* loved.

It was Michele, his boss and the woman he'd been seeing for two years, who had convinced him to take the promotion. Blackmailed him, really. That's not to say that he hadn't wanted the promotion; he'd worked hard for it, but ultimately it was Michele who was the deciding factor in his decision.

Their affair had started off innocently enough: a look here, a little flirting there. But since they'd spent so much time together, working long hours and traveling often, it quickly progressed. Michele had asked him one night on a business trip if he wanted to join her in her room for sex, and he'd said yes. It was easy—simple— so simple that one word and one poor decision altered the course of his life. Michele was older than he was, in her mid-forties and, as it turned out, savvier, too. She steered Patrick's career, which helped him climb the ladder quicker than anyone expected, least of all himself. So, it's safe to say, that what had started out as an innocent affair quickly became something more.

In fact, the situation snowballed so fast that, before long, he couldn't find his way out of it. While Michele wasn't as attractive as his wife and the sex only mediocre, Patrick found that he'd come to love her in his own way. She made it easy for him. *Or was it difficult?* He couldn't figure out which. When he really thought about why he hadn't put an end to the affair he realized that he was attracted, perhaps even addicted, to her power. But it was a love-hate relationship at best. She'd made Patrick dependent on her, his career dependent on her. And that was dangerous.

He hated lying to his wife. But he'd become good at it. There were a few times he thought that maybe she'd suspected, but she never called him on it, even though there were times when he hoped that she would. Not that he made it easy. Over the last two years, he'd become an expert liar. It helped that he was paranoid and moody, while Addison's attention was mostly focused on the children. He had purposely allowed more of the family responsibilities to fall on her shoulders, if nothing else to keep her occupied and out of his business.

Still, if he could make one thing clear it would be that just because he was seeing Michele, didn't mean he didn't love his wife. He loved her beyond measure. He just couldn't stop what he was doing was all. Michele was a persuasive woman. He knew this because the few times he had tried to end things between them, she knew exactly which threats to make to put an end to his requests. She had him by the balls, and they both knew it.

Patrick understood she wanted him to leave his wife. But his father had always made one thing clear, do your thing on the side if you wanted, but Greyer men don't just up and leave their families. Keeping a mistress was one thing, but a man who walked out on his family was another matter altogether. So, in the end, Michele did what he figured any smart woman would do and got him as far away from his family as possible. She concocted the expansion to China and put together a team that placed her and Patrick in starring roles, threatening to tell his wife if he stayed. He had hoped that Addison would've put up a bigger fight and given him an ultimatum. If she had, Patrick swore that he might even tell her the truth, knowing full well that it would cost him his career. The problem was the truth would cause him to lose his family, too.

Patrick came to hate the position he was in. He hated his job. He hated China. He hated Michele. His wife was in Italy on business, and there was nothing he could've done to stop her from going. Ever since she'd taken the job, he'd felt a shift. He felt things changing between them. Maybe it was nothing more than his own guilt talking, but he swore it was the beginning of the end.

~

SCOTT HAMMONS WOKE up on the beautiful Isle of Capri in a better mood than he'd been in, in a long, long time. The birds were chirping and the sun was shining. It was one of those days he just knew was going to be absolutely perfect. The day had finally come. He was over the moon.

Once and for all, he was going to put it all behind him, finally get the revenge he deserved. That bastard William Hartman had taken everything from him. Now it was his turn to take it all back. And then some. The time had come for William to pay up. One can't just swindle a man's life right out from under him and get away with it. William Hartman had taken his business, tearing it to shreds, selling it off piece by piece until there was nothing left. Scott's grandfather and great-grandfather had spent their entire lives building that business. And now it was gone. Sold to someone who didn't give a shit about the blood, sweat, and tears it had taken to build it. William Hartman was pure evil, sent by Lucifer himself, and he was going to get what had been coming to him.

Hartman had taken everything from him: not just his business, but his livelihood, and even his family. He'd caused Scott to become what he was: an old drunkard consumed by hate. An eye for an eye, Scott decided, because everyone knew what the Bible said: *"If a man shall deliver unto his neighbor money or stuff to keep, and it be stolen out of the man's house; if the thief be found, let him pay double."* Hartman had stolen from him, and now he needed to know what it was like to suffer. And boy would he ever suffer. Then he would die. This was the only way because the Bible said, *"Thou shall not steal."* And Hartman had stolen from him. He'd taken everything there was to take. He'd broken God's law. Now, he needed to repent. He needed to give his life the way Scott had. Scott would make sure the process wasn't pleasant, not at all. He would see to it William experienced a slow and painful death, just the way he had as he watched as everything was slowly taken from him: His wife and children. The family business. He knew that people talked about him, said he squandered it away with his drinking. Lies! All lies! No doubt started by Hartman himself just so he could take and take and take. But the Bible said: *"Lying lips are an abomination to the Lord, but those who act faithfully are his delight."* Hartman was a liar and Scott would fix that. William Hartman was the devil and Scott realized he may not have been able to save his business or his family but he could still do the Lord's work.

Plus, Scott knew he was a smart man, no matter what others said about him. He knew what had to be done. He'd always taken care of business, despite what Hartman and the evildoers said. This time was no different. Once he signed away the last of his business, once he had signed away what remained of his life, he decided to do what any gracious man of God would do and invite that prick to lunch on his yacht to celebrate.

Scott would show him. First, he was going to slip a little something into his drink, make him a little drowsy, and then he'd make him pay. God's will would be done. And since the Lord himself had spoken to Scott and told him exactly the plan of action to take, he was well prepared. God had said to tie him up. God told Scott to cut Hartman's tongue out prior to killing him because Hartman was a liar. And that's what he deserved. This way, he'd never be able to lie again. The Bible said: *"Keep your tongue from evil and your lips from speaking deceit."* Then once that was taken care of, God had instructed Scott to cut off his greedy little fingers because the Bible said: *"A greedy man brings trouble to his family, but he who hates bribes will live."*

Scott couldn't wait to watch William beg for his life. Scott would please his Heavenly Father, and He would smile down upon him, happy with his work. And in turn for his obedience, God would give him his life back. After all, when you did the Lord's work, you were in His favor and Scott desperately needed to be in His favor.

What Scott didn't plan for was having that pretty little bitch accompany Hartman to lunch. Not only was he taken by surprise, he was infuriated. Now, he'd have to kill her, too. The other problem was Hartman also had in tow three more members of his security team than Scott had planned for. *Damn it! This wasn't in the plan. Why hadn't God warned him about this?* Scott slapped himself over and over. *Stupid. Stupid. Stupid. You are such a fuck up! Think. Think. Think.*

He downed three glasses of gin and suddenly felt better.

He went on with the lunch, abandoning God's will for now, but as upset as Scott was, he was grateful. He knew the Bible said: *"We do not want you to become lazy, but to imitate those who, through faith and patience, inherit what has been promised."* It turned out that the Lord gave him an incredible gift that day. For years, he had been plotting and planning his revenge against William Hartman. But since Hartman was the devil incarnate, there were few things he loved—few things other than destroying people's lives, that is. God sent him a sign that day on the boat. Scott finally found something that Hartman loved just as much as Scott loved his family and his business—the family and the business that William had taken from him. He could see it clear as day, Hartman was in love with this girl.

The day that Scott Hammons met Addison Greyer, he hit the jackpot. He finally understood what his Heavenly Father wanted. The Lord wanted to teach him patience. He wanted him to wait, to lurk in the shadows. And when the time was right, He wanted Scott to take away the one thing that William Hartman loved. And when God spoke, he listened.

WILLIAM SIPPED his champagne from the deck intrigued by the way Addison interacted with Scott Hammons. He watched, as she seemed to crack him, breaking him out of his shell. She was a natural. Scott Hammons was more talkative and friendlier than William had ever seen him.

Still, William had reservations about bringing her along. He knew better than to mix business with pleasure. But he also knew he wanted her to be a part of his life, and business was a large part of who he was. So, he beefed-up security and consulted with his team before making the decision. There was something about Scott that put him off. William didn't

trust him. For starters, Scott Hammons was an odd character, although the three liters of gin he was known to
consume daily likely contributed to that. He was known to
be reclusive and strange in the business world, and William
had always felt a little bit sorry for him—although not sorry
enough to walk away from a good business deal. Business
was business.

Suffice it to say, it was a pleasure to see Scott and Addison
getting along so well. William watched him laugh at something Addison had said and wondered if there was anything
about her that wasn't absolutely perfect. *That's how you know.*

Addison Greyer had made him happier than he'd ever
been. And it seemed that she had that effect on others, too.
William decided then and there, on that boat, that he
couldn't let this one slip away. He promised himself he would
do whatever it took. He would bury his past. Put it behind
him. He would finally learn how to love and be loved in
return because this one was a keeper. Just then, she looked
up, caught his eye, and winked at him. He smiled, unable to
take his eyes off of her, unable to focus on anything but how
beautiful she was. And for the first time in his life, William
Hartman understood what it felt like to be in love.

CHAPTER FOURTEEN

Addison returned home from Italy, anxious to see her boys. Having never been away from them, she hadn't realized it possible to miss them *that* much.

The day after she returned, she spent the entire day watching them swim and run and play and chase Max in their backyard. It was a gorgeous day, the kind that made all your worries suddenly seem insignificant. She wanted to stop time, to bottle it up and make her boys stay this way forever with their moppy heads and little boy smells.

The following morning, she returned to work, wishing she'd taken another day or two off. Unfortunately, her inbox was overflowing, and there were several proposals she needed to get out. Even so, she planned on leaving the office early to catch up on lost time with the kids.

Patrick had called the night before, and Addison could swear she heard something in his voice that sounded uneasy. She knew it would be hard having him so far away, but she hadn't really thought it would be *this* hard. The distance between them was beginning to set in, in a way it never had before. Still, she was angry with Patrick for accepting the assignment in China, which is in part, she realized, what fueled the affair with William. Worse, she missed her husband and all the while hated to admit that she was beginning to understand his decision on some level. Patrick loved his work. It was who he was. With a little time and perspective, and albeit guilt, she couldn't help but feel a sense of compassion towards him for wanting to provide for his family by climbing the corporate ladder.

Upon her return to the office, Addison opened her office door to find three vases full of purple orchids sitting on her desk. She smiled, opening the card.

Dear Addison,

Thank you for giving my life color. I hope each time you look at these you'll think of me and the three beautiful days we spent together in Italy.

I miss you.

Yours,
William

She wondered what William was thinking, sending her flowers at the office. *Again*. Anyone could've read the card. And there would certainly be a lot of questions each time one of her colleagues entered her office. *Damn him.* She had to fix this. She had to figure something out and fast. But for now, she had work to do.

Trying to take her mind off of the situation, she typed up a few proposals and then started on the 312 emails sitting in her inbox. Only one of them grabbed her attention and held it.

From: William B. Hartman

Date: 6/25/2012

To: Addison Greyer

Subject: I Miss You

Dearest Addison,

I hope you like the flowers.

Words can't describe how much I miss waking up next to you in the morning.

Your presence gives my life new meaning. And your absence leaves a noticeable void. Tell me, "What is a man to do?"

I need to see you before it all goes further downhill. ;)

A car will be waiting outside the lobby at noon. Go outside and get in it. I'll be waiting.

See you soon.

Kisses,

William

She read the email twice and then sighed glancing at the clock. Eleven forty-five. Crap. Didn't he know that the rest of the world actually had to work for a living?

Admittedly, she'd spent a little extra time on her hair and makeup just in case she might run into him. So, why then was she so surprised? Still, she had to admit she wanted to see William, too. But more so, she realized it was time she put a stop to the flowers and the emails. That's why, she did as she was told, and at twelve o'clock sharp, hopped in the car that drove her to his place.

Addison had second thoughts as she rode the elevator up.

What was she doing here? This has to stop. It's only going to end badly...

William opened the door, wearing faded blue jeans and a crisp white button-down shirt. *Casual. Especially for him.*

She grinned as he moved to the side and ushered her in. "Working today?"

"Always," William said as he bent down, kissing her on the cheek.

Addison glanced around the place, noticing how different it felt from her own home. How quiet and lonely it seemed. She folded her arms. "So, you got me here. Now what?"

"Oh, so it's like that now?" he asked, using his body to push her up against the wall. They hadn't even made it out of the foyer. He kissed her nose and brushed a strand of hair away from her eye. "This dress is . . . I must say . . . very nice, but I'm afraid it's going to have to come off," he said, his hands trailing lower, slowly making their way down the length of her torso.

Addison shook her head. Then she reached up and ran her fingers through his hair, curling a strand around her finger, tugging gently. "You think so, do you?"

He nodded and then unzipped her dress. She watched it fall to the floor. This is what she'd come here for. She realized that now. *It was good to feel wanted.* Since there was no turning back now, she pushed William to the floor and straddled him, slowly moving up and down.

He sighed, whispering in her ear. "I need you, Addison."

Finishing in unison, they both lay on the floor, Addison's head on his chest. William's fingers traced the outline of her face until eventually she sat up and stared down at him. "God you're beautiful," he said.

Addison smirked, "I don't know what it was I came here for, but I guess that'll do."

The corners of his lips tilted slightly. "I'm glad you came."

"I'm glad I came, too," she smiled, raising her brow.

"That's my girl."

"I shall come again." Addison smirked, pulling her dress up.

William stared. "That's my job."

She shook her head and then pulled herself up, catching a glimpse of her reflection in the mirror on the way up. She couldn't help but notice that the girl staring back at her looked happy. Carefree.

William stood and fastened his jeans. "Stay a while. You hungry?"

"I can't. I'm sorry," she told him, looking away. "I gotta get back to work."

William feigned disappointment. "Seriously? You're just going to use me and run?"

"For now. Yes."

"Hmmm."

"Things are a bit crazy at work," she said, kissing his cheek.

He watched her walk toward the door. "I'll have lunch sent to your office. It'll be waiting when you get back." William told her, opening the door.

Addison met his eye, trying to avoid the range of emotions she was feeling. Trying and failing to keep the situation light. "Thank you, William."

He nodded once and then pulled her in and held her face in place while he kissed her the way he wanted. "Thank *you*," he finally said, releasing her.

~

ADDISON RETURNED to her office to find Sondra waiting for her. *Shit.*

Sondra stood as Addison closed the door behind her.

When Addison turned, she couldn't help but notice Sondra's disheveled appearance. She looked . . . terrible . . . unlike herself.

Great. I'm getting fired.

Sondra motioned towards a chair. "Take a seat, Addison."

She did as she was told.

Sondra took a deep breath. "I was expecting to see you in my office this morning."

"I know and I'm sorry," Addison started and then paused folding her hands in her lap. "I just had a lot to catch up on and..."

Sondra eyed her up and down in a way that told her she wasn't fooling anyone. "Yeah," she told her, shaking her head. "It looks that way."

Addison glanced around her office; looking for a way out of the hole she'd just dug herself into. "What can I do for you?"

Sondra picked up a stack of papers from Addison's desk and fanned herself. "I want to know if you've made a decision in regard to my offer?"

"I . . . Uh . . . Yes," Addison started to say but the answer seemed to be lodged somewhere deep inside. She cleared her throat and recovered. "I've given it a lot of thought and I so appreciate you thinking of me, but—"

Sondra raised her hand in the air, cutting her off. "I'm pregnant, Addison, exactly eight weeks along and, if you can't tell—" she said looking down at the floor. "I'm sicker than I've ever been in my life."

Addison tried to keep her face neutral. "Wow. Congratulations."

Sondra inhaled slowly and let it out. "Let me finish—"

Addison chewed on her bottom lip. "Sorry."

"I've been doing this for a very long time, and I have built an extensive and exclusive list of clientele. Clearly, I cannot continue to see my clients throughout this pregnancy."

Addison nodded. "I imagine not."

"The real kicker is that I never expected to be able to have children. Not ever. Everyone said it was impossible given my history. And to tell you the truth, I've never really cared much about being a mother," Sondra told her with a heavy sigh. "But now that it's happened, well, I've given it a lot of thought, and I figure, what the hell, I might as well embrace it."

"You're right. Your profession and babies don't exactly mix very well," Addison agreed unsure of what the correct response should be. "What about the father? Will he be involved?"

She shook her head. "No. He won't. But we'll be fine."

"I see."

"That's why I'm just going to cut to the chase. Dungeon Seven is my life, and I cannot just step out of it without losing my clients. They're accustomed to a certain level of service."

"I'm sure they are but—"

"Addison—I've given this a lot of thought. I need *you*. And I need you to say yes."

She tilted her head. "You don't even know me..."

"I know enough. Probably more than you think. That's my job, you see. And sure, yes... there are other Dommes out there that I could farm these clients out to, but to be frank, I just don't feel comfortable doing it. I want someone who I can trust and who is specifically trained by me. With the proper amount of training, I know, without a doubt you'd be perfect. So, what is it? Is it the money? Because—"

"Fine," Addison blurted out, cutting Sondra off. "I'll do it."

Sondra smiled, slowly.

Addison exhaled, her mind had wandered to her own

children, and, somehow, the words just slipped out. She walked to the floor to ceiling window and stared out at the skyline. Eventually, she sighed. She wasn't sure why, but saying yes just felt right, in spite of her reservations. She glanced over her shoulder at Sondra who looked relieved. "But I expect a signing bonus."

Sondra stood and walked towards the door, smiling. "You got it. I'll have my assistant get everything in place and we'll work on getting your household fully staffed. This is going to demand your full attention. Your training begins tomorrow at five a.m. sharp."

She grimaced. "Five a.m.?"

"Yeah, is that a problem?"

"Well—"

"Addison—this is no joke. I want to be very clear about that. We need to whip your ass into shape," Sondra warned, eyeing her from head to toe. "Literally. This line of work is incredibly physical..."

She nodded, hoping she hadn't just made the biggest mistake of her life.

ADDISON WOKE to her phone ringing at four a.m. It was her new chef asking to be let in. She climbed out of bed. *Jesus, what had her life become.*

Over breakfast, she was informed that she was only to eat what the chef, an older man named Alexander, who as it turned out was Russian, prepared. Addison was instructed that he must approve all food. She was carefully schooled on the strict diet, which only allowed her to consume a limited number of calories in order to stay within the regimen Alexander prepared.

But if Addison thought Alexander was a ball buster, she

couldn't have been less prepared for the trainer who showed up promptly at four forty-five a.m. Andre was brutal. He wore her out in the first five minutes, yet insisted she complete the entire hour-long training session. It was pure hell and she wanted to quit. In fact, she planned on it. *What had she gotten herself into?*

Addison showered and was surprised to find the boys happily chatting with Alexander when she came back downstairs. Kelsey, the nanny, had already arrived.

"Hey, Mrs. Greyer," she said cheerfully. Kelsey was one of those perpetually happy people, who never seemed to have anything bad to say. "I just wanted to thank you. I LOVE my new schedule. I mean... I can't tell you how much this will help towards my student loans, not to mention I just really love your kids."

Addison smiled, kissing each of the boys. "I'm happy you're happy and I know a trio of boys who feel the same way about you."

Addison sat watching them eat as Kelsey packed lunches. *Maybe this was a good thing after all.* It would give her back to them. Instead of trying to do everything herself as a single mom, at least now she had a team in place.

AFTER SHE SAW the boys off to school, Addison was picked up by a car service and driven downtown to the warehouse district where Dungeon Seven was located. Seven as it was called was in an unassuming building that could've easily passed as any ol' inconspicuous office. The entrance was freshly decorated and bright, complete with a cheerful receptionist.

"You must be Addison."

"Yes."

"I'm Liselle."

The girl rose from behind the desk and ushered Addison towards a door on her right. "Ms. Sheehan asked that you step into this room and dress in the clothing hanging there on the rack," she told Addison pointing. "She'll greet you momentarily."

Addison nodded and watched as Liselle closed the door behind her. Touching the outfit hanging before her, she couldn't help but laugh. *Seriously?* She ran her fingers over the leather catsuit. It looked like something straight out of Hollywood.

She scowled, twisted and turned, struggling to pull the tight leather over her body. Already sore from Andre's crazy intense workout, it didn't make it easy. Baby powder helped and once it was finally on, it fit like a glove, and was surprisingly comfortable. Addison eyed herself in the full-length mirror, pleased and a little amused with what she saw. *What a long way she had come. What a long way still to go.* She slipped the six-inch heels on that had been left for her and checked the mirror again. The woman in the mirror staring back looked fierce. Not like her at all. Satisfied, she picked up the client profile and studied it, testing herself to make sure she'd memorized every last detail.

The gentleman named "Thomas" was a forty-five-year-old surgeon. He had fantasies of being forced to dress female, ridiculed, and spanked. Sondra listed specific names that were to be used during the session, specifically, "Pussy" and "Freak Boy."

She heard the door open and in walked Sondra wearing a corset, fishnets and leather boots. Addison sat up straighter. *How was it possible that the woman always looked so good, even more so dressed like this?*

Sondra gave her the once over, finally giving a sly smile. "Not bad."

Addison felt her face flush and her stomach flip, suddenly feeling anxious and awkward. If she wanted out, now was her chance.

"Thomas will be in, in a moment."

Addison swallowed hard, her pulse pounding in her ears.

"Just watch me and don't speak unless spoken to. That's all you're here for this time. Just to observe. So, relax. Once we're done with the session, I'll instruct you on technique and we'll review. Any questions?"

Addison shook her head slightly.

Thomas was not at all what she had expected. He was handsome and surprisingly normal-looking. Sondra introduced Addison as Mistress Laelia. *Funny, they hadn't agreed on that name, but Addison decided she kind of liked it.* Thomas kissed her hand when she extended it. Out of nowhere came the first blow.

"I didn't give you permission to kiss Mistress Laelia. Did I?" Sondra struck Thomas again as he hung his head. "DID I?"

Sondra bent next to his ear and whispered. "You're nothing but a dumb little pussy wimp who can't even follow simple instructions. You think you're so smart having people refer to you as Doctor. Don't you?" She shouted. Addison winced. She couldn't help herself. Sondra went on. "But you're not. You're a fraud. And everyone knows it. You stupid little shit."

Thomas remained quiet, his eyes focused on the floor.

Sondra put her hands around his neck and began squeezing as Addison watched the flesh turn red, the blood pool. "Look at me when I speak to you!"

Thomas looked up at Sondra, his eyes glazed over. "No girl clothes today, huh? What do you think, you're *too* good? Who do you think you are, huh? Running around thinking you're better than everyone else."

His expression was blank. He was somewhere else. Sondra backhanded him once again. And this went on and on for nearly an hour until Sondra removed the collar and Thomas stood, smiled, and kissed her on the cheek. It was like he'd checked out through the entirety of it, and then when it was all said and done, he came back to himself, elation playing across his face.

He beamed, a different man than only minutes before. "See you next week."

"Yes. Next week."

After the session, Addison wasn't elated. She was drained. Sondra went over technique with her on proper ways of punishing without leaving marks. They did two more sessions that day, each much like the last, only different faces and different names. When they were finished, they changed clothes: Addison into a fitted knee-length skirt and matching blouse; Sondra into a pantsuit. From there, they grabbed lunch and headed to the agency, like normal, as though nothing out of the ordinary had just taken place.

In the elevator, Addison cocked her head to one side and studied Sondra. "Laelia? It's interesting… I've never heard it before. I like it."

Sondra smiled wryly. "It means Orchid. I hear they're your favorite flowers."

She deadpanned. "So they say."

OVER THE FOLLOWING WEEK, Addison continued training with Sondra until she'd seen all of the six clients who would be in her rotation. There was the surgeon who enjoyed cross dressing, the professor who wanted to be chained and disciplined by a cheerleader for daring to look at her, the attorney who enjoyed being treated like a dog but preferred limited corporal punishment, the corporate CEO with a foot fetish, the writer who dressed like a boy scout and enjoyed being tied up and gagged while ridiculed about his inadequacies as a man, and the concert pianist who asked to be chained and spanked by his teacher for being a bad boy and breaking the rules.

Each session went much like the last. Over the course of the week, Addison had undergone intensive sessions on knot tying with rope, martial arts, sensory deprivation, the use of hot wax, the art of using corporal punishment without leaving marks not limited to: whips, floggers, and canes, and the proper way to perform a choke hold. She learned first aid, CPR, discipline therapy, and fantasy development. Interestingly enough, the hardest part of it all was the extremely intense workout sessions with Andre. He not only broke her physically but mentally, as well. There were days where she could barely walk, let alone keep herself mentally prepared and focused on the work to be done. Sondra assured her though, that once the initial training was complete, life as a Mistress, while still demanding and technical and required that one be vigilant at all times, was mostly a matter of acting. She just needed to tune into her client's needs, play the part, and the rest, Sondra assured her, would fall into place.

Despite her exhaustion and cravings, thanks to the new diet, she was finding life at home was easier than it had been when Patrick first left. The boys seemed to be thriving with all of the new people around the house. While their home had become lonely and sad after Patrick left, it was now vibrant again and bustling. It helped that she was becoming more confident and fit by the day, in control of her life, finally she seemed able to stand on her own two feet. Her newly found confidence spilled over to life at the office as well. Her colleagues took notice and began coming to her for advice, and the new clients were pouring in.

Addison wasn't purposely trying to avoid William, but he apparently saw things differently and showed up unexpectedly in her office one morning, startling her, as once again, she walked in to find him sitting at her desk. "Goddammit," she said, glancing out the door to see who was around. She didn't want to be seen with him. She knew how people talked.

"Nice to see you, too," he said, condescendingly.

Addison folded her arms and leaned against the door. "What the hell is wrong with you? You can't just barge in here like this anytime you damn well please."

"*Au contraire.* I can do as I damn well please. I own this building, remember?"

She walked over to her desk and perched herself on the edge. She was so close she could smell his aftershave, so close she felt more than she wanted to. Still, she needed to get her point across. "Well, you don't own me, and I don't particularly appreciate your lack of boundaries," she told him nodding toward the door. "So, get out."

William eyed her up and down, grinning. "Have you been working out?"

Shit. He was good. "Seriously, William, get out!"

He looked around the office and glanced at his Rolex, his face pained. "Well, if you won't talk to me now, then tell me, when *is* a better time for you?'"

Her heart sank. "I'll have my assistant call yours and set something up later in the week."

William threw his head back and laughed a little too loud. "Oh, so it's like that now?"

She rolled her eyes and put much needed space between them before she did something she'd regret. "We're both busy, William."

He stood and stared into her eyes for a second longer than made her comfortable, then he nodded. "I see. Look—if you want to play hard to get, fine. I'll play all day long. But something tells me that's not what this is. I know how to play dirty," he said and paused to adjust his suit jacket. "And I'm well prepared to do so, if that's what it takes."

"Nice."

William scoffed. "I didn't get where I am today by playing nice. You should keep that in mind."

Addison shook her head. *Jesus.* William glanced at her one more time, then brushed by her, before turning back and placing a kiss to her temple. She flinched involuntarily and he sighed. "This is not the way this was supposed to go," he said and then he took two short strides to the door, closing it harder than necessary.

Addison sank down into her chair, still warm from where he'd been. She gasped, trying to catch her breath. Both infuriated and thrilled by the effect that man had on her, she couldn't help but smile just a little. *God, she was so fucked.*

TRUE TO HIS WORD, William Hartman played hardball and showed up on Addison's schedule the following day. Her assistant pointed out that he'd requested a three-hour block of time, forcing her to cancel and rearrange her entire day. When Addison asked her why she'd done it and informed her never to do it again, the poor girl looked confused as though she had lost her mind. "It was William Hartman calling."

Addison smiled wryly. "Mr. Hartman doesn't get three hours of my day. Please call my two o'clock back and tell them we're still on and then please let Mr. Hartman know that I had to cut our meeting short by an hour."

The girl looked at her as though she'd grown two heads. "Will do."

Addison met Carl at the SUV waiting just outside the lobby at eleven o'clock. When it took off in a different direction, she eyed his reflection in the rearview mirror. He seemed to know what she was going to ask. "Mr. Hartman says to tell you you're in for a change of scenery today, Mrs. Greyer."

She frowned. *Oh, he did, did he?*

They arrived at the W Hotel via a private entrance and entered a private elevator that delivered her to the penthouse suite where William was waiting dressed in his usual Armani suit. He never deviated. Not in color and not in brand. She'd been meaning to ask him why.

Instead, she looked around the place and then finally met his gaze. "What is *this*?"

He grinned and held his palms out, face up. "It's the penthouse, baby."

Addison closed the gap between the two of them, standing inches from his face. "Yeah, I can see that. Why am I here?"

William ran his hands over her shoulders and down her arms, stopping at her wrists. Chills ran through her as he squeezed hard, cutting off the blood flow. "Like I said . . . I'm finished playing nice. I figured you wanted to be treated like the others."

Addison flung her wrists down fast, surprising William and causing him to release her. She cocked her head and narrowed her eyes. "The others?"

"Yeah, the women I bring here. To fuck," he snapped, scowling.

She shot him a look that could kill and took one step backward. "Wow, you're a fucking genius. And since you've got me all figured out, which way to the bed? We'd better hurry..."

He stepped towards her and pushed her back to the wall, subduing her with his body, holding her in place. He ran his hands down the length of her, slipping his fingers underneath her dress. "Who needs a bed?" he glared.

The next twenty minutes contained the most intense sex of her life. They did make it to the bed, actually, where William proceeded to punish her in ways she hadn't known possible, taking her to the edge and bringing her back, again and again. In turn, she clawed and bit, until, in the end, they were both exhausted, depleted.

William stood eventually, walked away, and came back with a glass of water. He shoved it in her direction. "Drink."

Addison sat up and sipped the water. "Thank you."

William lifted her wrist, inspecting the red marks. Frowning, he rubbed his fingers in circles over them, bringing them to his lips and gently kissing each one. "Oh yeah," he said eventually. "So, this is what it takes?"

She cocked her head to the side and rubbed her chin. *Keep it light.* "Yeah. Maybe."

He grabbed her chin, forcing her to look at him. "I've missed you, Addison."

"I'm sorry. But I have a family and a job and... I've been busy. Things are crazy at work and the boys keep me on my toes all day long."

William couldn't help but notice the way her face lit up when she talked about her children.

"I'd like to meet them," he said, lowering his voice, searching her eyes.

She pressed her lips together. "I don't think that's a good idea."

"Is it ever going to be a good idea?"

"I don't know," she replied flatly.

"You know what I think, Addison? I think you have no

intention of taking things any further than they are right now. That's why I brought you here. That's why I fucked you the way I just did. Because if this is the way you want it, then you need to just say so. But first— you should know that I love you. I want to be with you. I want more. I want to take care of you," he told her, his expression intense. "You just have to let me."

A thousand thoughts ran through her head. She couldn't keep up. Mostly, she didn't know what to say. *He wants more? More than this? What would happen if she let her guard down?* In that moment, she didn't have the answers. So, Addison did the only thing she knew to do to protect herself. She shrugged her shoulders, kept a straight face and lied. "This is the way I want it."

LATER THAT EVENING, she arrived home exhausted. She had agreed to a late session with Sondra and a client in a few hours but wanted to see the boys and shower first. Only as she was finding more and more often as of late, things rarely go as planned.

Addison froze as she shut the door behind her. Her breath caught at the sight of Patrick sitting on the couch, looking smug, as though he'd never left. He glanced at the clock on the wall. "You're late," he said.

Her stomach sank. "What are you doing home?" she asked straining her neck toward the kitchen. "Where are the boys?"

He stood and walked over to her. She stepped back instinctively.

"Well, nice to see you, too," Patrick said, leaning in for a kiss. She could smell the liquor on his breath.

"I'm sorry. But why don't you start by telling me what's going on?" she hissed, turning her cheek.

He grabbed her as she tried to move away and pulled her close, his breath hot on her neck. "I guess I could ask you the same."

She pushed against his chest. Hard. "Where are the kids, Patrick?"

He put his hands up in surrender. "Relax. They're with my mom. She picked me up at the airport and wanted to give us some time."

Addison eyed him skeptically. "Time for what?"

Patrick sat back down on the sofa and kicked his feet up. "I don't know. Time to get reacquainted."

"What are you doing home?" she asked, rubbing her temples.

"You're not happy to see me?"

"That's not what I said… it's unexpected is all."

"My mother called, she thought it was time I came home. That and you haven't been answering my calls lately. I guess I just needed to see that you're ok." Patrick told her. Then he leaned back, folded his hands behind his head, and studied her. "And my God, Addie, are you ever ok. You're amazing. So, tell me… what in the hell have you been up to?" he asked and he slurred his words as he spoke. "Because whatever it is, it sure looks good on you."

Addison didn't miss a beat. "I finally wised up and got some help around here," she answered, served up with a go-fuck-yourself smile.

CHAPTER FIFTEEN

With Patrick home, Addison was going insane trying to manage the web of lies that she had spun. She had to be extra careful, she realized, upon learning that her mother-in-law thought something was up and had called Patrick home. Patrick wouldn't let on what he thought was going on, saying only that he missed her and the kids and wanted a break. But she knew better. *Penny Greyer loved to stir up trouble, especially where Addison was concerned.*

Sondra had been furious when she'd had to cancel on her the other night, but after seeing that Addison still intended to see the deal through, Sondra relented and together they concocted a plan. Addison's assistant would arrive each morning and go over her schedule with her, making sure that Patrick was within earshot. She and Sondra would then have a conference call to discuss the day's events, again within earshot of her husband. This way when she was late coming and going, he understood, or thought he understood why. As horrible as she felt about deceiving Patrick this way, she figured it was only short term. Just until she figured out a *real* plan. Or until he left again.

Of course, it helped that she and Patrick had rekindled things, calling an unspoken truce. He couldn't keep his hands off of her, and Addison cooled a little. All of her deception helped with that. To her surprise, once her bases were covered, she found herself enjoying having him home, especially given how happy the boys were.

But all of the lying and the covering up meant that she had absolutely no energy or attention to give William or his emails. She'd texted him, letting him know that Patrick was home, and he'd responded with an email which Addison couldn't bring herself to open. After their last exchange at the W, she felt that something had broken, and she wasn't sure how to put it back together. Worse yet, she wasn't sure whether or not it was even possible to do so. Or whether she wanted to.

On the fourth day, Addison found William in her office, once again, sitting at her desk. This time, she wasn't all that surprised to see him sitting there. It took a moment for him to look up, and she was confused, certain he'd heard her, until she noticed what he was holding: *her family photo.*

She watched the way he studied it as she made her way over to the desk. She eyed him intently but said nothing.

He cleared his throat. "You know... the funny thing is... I've never walked away from anything before. If I wanted it, that is. But I'm willing to do it . . .this time, for you."

He placed the picture back in its place and held his gaze on it. "For them, I guess, would be a better way to put it."

She reached for his hand and curled his fingers in hers. "I'm sorry," she whispered, surprised that she'd lost her voice. "It's just that the timing for us is all sorts of wrong."

His voice deepened. "Don't bullshit me, Addison," he warned. "That's the one thing I ask. Give it to me straight. I've played this game myself, too many times to count, so I know it when I see it."

Her hand recoiled. "I'm not toying with you, and I'm not sure what it is exactly that you're asking," she told him. "But I'm pretty sure it's more than I can give."

He shook his head and then scoffed. "I'm asking for you to give me a shot. Give *us* a shot. Do you have any idea how great we could be together?"

Addison stood and walked toward the window. "You don't even know what you're asking," she said, eventually. "I'm married with *three* children," she added, turning to face him. "You have no idea what that's like. We live completely different lives. Meeting up and having carefree sex doesn't make a relationship."

He looked her dead in the eye. "I never implied that it did."

"Then what exactly *are* you implying?" she asked, placing her hands on her hips.

He leaned back in the chair and swallowed hard before answering. "I'm asking you to make a decision. I'm asking whether you want to give this a shot. If you do, then great— give me your stipulations— and I'll give you mine. If you don't, then fine, but let me know and—" he paused to make quotations in the air. "And we'll end all of this 'carefree sex' we've been having."

Addison wanted to go to him. She wanted to ease the pain she saw written all over his face, but she couldn't let herself. In the end, she realized, they would both wind up hurt. No matter how badly she wanted to utter the words and instantly make it all better, she wouldn't. She knew this was coming. She'd thought it over, she'd considered her children and Patrick and what it would do to them if she gave into this. She'd already decided what she'd say. There were too many lives at stake, *too* many people who'd get caught in the crossfire. *Too many secrets to keep.* So, she did what she had to do and mouthed the words that she knew would bring him

177

to his knees and end it all. "I love my husband. I need to see it through. I'm sorry."

He visibly flinched. He stood and hesitated for a second, staring at the floor before he quietly walked toward the door. When he got to the doorway, he stopped, stood up a little straighter, and smiled. "Well then, I guess I'll see you around."

It took everything she had not to go to him, not to tell him the truth. She wanted him to know that he'd made her happier in these past few weeks than she'd ever been. But she didn't. Instead she just pressed her lips to one another and watched as he turned and walked away.

Fuck Addison Greyer. He'd show her. William decided to call up every woman in his contact list that he'd ever slept with and made arrangements. Hell, he'd already gone through three of them in the last twenty-four hours alone. It wasn't much but it was the best he could come up with. He planned to sleep her right off his mind.

After a week in a sex-fueled haze, William felt better, though a little worse for the wear. He had used his anger to fuel a few major business deals, and nothing made him happier than money. *Nothing except Addison Greyer.*

He *had* to get her off of his mind. So, William threw himself into his work. After a week or so when that didn't work, he called up one of his favorite girls and flew the two of them out to Vegas. Sin City would do the trick; he was sure of it.

Patrick understood that he'd have to head back to China. He'd told Michele that one of the boys was sick, but he knew he couldn't lie forever. Luckily, he'd been able to push his trip out to two weeks, and, quite frankly, he wasn't ready to leave even then.

First off, things between him and Addison were going so well. There was something about her that had changed while he was away. She was stronger, *different*, more attractive than before, which was funny because, even though he hadn't thought he would, he liked her that way.

Second, while his mother swore that something was going on, that his wife was falling apart, into drugs, or, worse yet, having an affair, Patrick hadn't seen any evidence of it. In fact, it was just the opposite. From what he could see, she'd been holding everything together perfectly. Still, he told Penny to keep an eye out. Just in case.

The two weeks he was home, he threw himself into fatherhood, making up for lost time. Patrick realized how much he had missed his kids, and that made him determined to convince Addison to move to China. He had no idea how he'd make the situation work with Michele but they'd done it back in the States, and so, they'd have to figure it out. He knew, eventually, that he'd have to end things with Michele but decided he needed another promotion and more time. After all, tomorrow he was headed back and it was nice to have someone waiting to comfort him.

THINGS FOR ADDISON had been hectic over the previous two weeks with her Domme training and having Patrick home. It was nice to have her family all together, but if she were honest with herself, she would admit that it would also be nice to see Patrick go, too. She needed a reprieve from all of the lying and the hiding. She loved seeing the boys so happy to have their father home, but she wanted to throw herself into her work and in many ways, Patrick reminded her of a fourth child. She told herself she was being selfish, but she felt it nonetheless.

Then there was the matter of William. She desperately wanted to see him. Not that she would. But she wanted to. It helped that with everything going on, there hadn't been the time. Plus, she was able to use her hurt and anger to fuel her work as a Domme. She bottled it up and used it on the men who called her Mistress. Thankfully, it seemed to be working; Sondra was getting stellar reviews.

The night before Patrick left, he and Addison lay awake in bed for a long while, talking about the future: their plans, their hopes, and their dreams. But later, when they made love, it was William's face she saw as she closed her eyes. It was William she dreamt of that night. She saw William surrounded by flames, calling her name. But no matter how hard she tried, she couldn't reach him. She tried to save him from the fire but she couldn't. All she could do was stand and watch as the flames engulfed his body. She awoke in the dark, panting and covered in sweat.

She grabbed her phone, climbed out of bed, went into the bathroom, and sat on the edge of the bathtub. She typed "William Hartman" into Google. The headline that popped up made her smile, though just a little. But not for long.

BILLIONAIRE PLAYBOY GAMBLES AWAY MILLIONS IN VEGAS.

The article was complete with pictures, which infuriated her. They showed an incredibly handsome William, complete with his signature shit-eating grin, surrounded by women and liquor. *All right, so he wasn't burning to death in a fiery hellhole.* He was in Vegas. She slammed her phone down and pinched the bridge of her nose. *Same difference.*

WILLIAM WAS SITTING in the office of the penthouse suite of Caesar's Palace when Carl came in wielding a file, thrusting it his way.

"I think it's time to go home, sir."

William looked at Carl, confused. "I think I'll be the judge of that. Thank you very much."

Carl spoke, his tone serious. "You need to have a look at what's in the file. Enough is enough."

William hesitated, and then opened the folder and pulled the contents out, spilling them on the desk. There were photos of a man and woman together intimately. William looked at Carl and shook his head. "What is this?"

"Sir, this is Patrick Greyer and his boss."

"His boss?"

"According to our sources, he's been seeing her for quite some time."

William leaned back in his chair, running his fingers through his hair. *Shit.* "Where did you get this?"

"May I?" Carl asked, before sitting in the chair adjacent to the desk.

William shrugged.

"Research, sir."

"But why?" William demanded, pinching the bridge of his nose and squeezing his eyes shut.

"Look at you. You're a mess. I've never seen you like this…"

"I'm fine."

"You're not fine. You're clearly in love with this girl. And unlike the others, from what little I know of her, I can see why."

"So?"

Carl sat up a little straighter. "So, I wanted to check her

out, see if she was worth the trouble. That's how I found this."

William stood and walked toward the windows, looking down at the hustle and bustle of the Vegas strip. "What is it you expect me to do with it?" he asked. "She made her decision."

"Based on a lie."

"I don't want that lie to be the reason she chooses otherwise, Carl," he replied, his tone harsh. "Don't you see? If she doesn't love me, showing her this isn't going to change that. And even if it did, it'd be for all the wrong reasons."

Carl remained neutral. "So, you're not going to tell her, then?"

William stayed quiet for a long time, so long that Carl thought maybe he hadn't heard him. Finally, when he spoke his voice was so quiet it was barely audible. "I can't hurt her like that. Clearly, she was doing the same thing, so who is to say she doesn't already know? It's quite possible she's even ok with it," he said.

William knew better, even before the words were out.

"Do you want me to do some more digging, sir? Find out?"

"No," William said, running his hand through his hair. "Let it be."

Carl stood. "Of course."

William turned from the window and looked Carl in the eye. "Oh, and Carl? Make sure that her name is never mentioned again. Understood?"

Carl nodded and shut the door behind him, certain of one thing. That night's events would be worse than any other.

CHAPTER SIXTEEN

Addison was rushing out the door when her cell phone rang. She dropped everything she was holding and searched for her phone, finally finding it in her pocket. Of course, it was Sondra. Who else would cause so much trouble at this hour?

"Morning Sondra," Addison said, breathless as she reached down to pick up her belongings.

"My God, who in their right mind sounds so chipper this early?"

Addison rolled her eyes. "Still not feeling any better?"

She sighed. "No. But listen, that's why I'm calling actually. I have a client I need you to see. This evening."

Perfect. She had some frustration that it wouldn't hurt to get out. "Ok."

"I was going to take this one myself, but this parasite that resides inside me isn't allowing me to stray too far from the nearest toilet bowl..."

Addison laughed.

Sondra did not. "They tell me it's a baby, but I'm not so sure."

"All right. I can handle it," Addison replied matter of factly.

"Here's the thing— " Sondra started to say, her tone harsh. "I need you to listen to me very carefully. And do exactly as I say. Do you understand?"

Addison picked up her cup and downed the last of her coffee. "Uh huh."

Sondra took a deep breath in and let it out. "This is serious, Addison. This one's important."

"Ok."

"You must stay in character and in charge at all times," Sondra warned. "No matter what. Do you understand?"

"Yes…"

"You have to promise me, because if you mess this one up, it's all over."

Addison rolled her eyes. *She's so dramatic.* "I understand."

"Good. I'll check in with you before the session," Sondra added. "I had Liselle pull his client profile. It's sitting on my desk at Seven. I also had her send for an outfit for you. This client prefers that a mask be worn. It's the number-one rule, ok?"

Addison checked the window. Her driver was waiting. "Great. Anything else I should know?"

"Just do as I say, ok? Stick to the rules. No matter what happens. That's the most important thing."

She sighed long and slow. "Will do." *That woman is so uptight.* Addison thought as she ended the call and flung the phone in her purse. *How in the world is she going to handle a kid?*

WHEN ADDISON GOT to the office, she called Liselle and asked her to courier the client's profile over so that she'd have plenty of time to read it beforehand. She wanted to go home and have dinner with the boys, so she'd need to get it done over lunch.

Liselle sounded annoyed. "I can't."

"Why not? You've sent stuff over before," Addison said, the irritation in her voice clear.

"Because this one is classified."

"Classified? Aren't they all?"

"Yes. But this one's particularly so," Liselle replied.

Addison massaged her temples. "Fine," she huffed. "I'll come over and get it myself."

"The file can't be removed from this office. As I said, it's classified."

She swallowed hard, trying to think of a solution. In the end, she realized there wasn't one. "Wonderful," she told Liselle, her tone seething. "I'll be over later."

Addison ended the call and slumped down in her chair. She knew she was frustrated but she hadn't realized she was this tense. As she closed her eyes, her thoughts instantly turned to William. She wondered what he was doing right now, and if he was thinking of her, too. She sat up and quickly typed the first part of his name in Google Search but stopped herself halfway through. *Let sleeping dogs lie.*

The rest of the morning flew by as she rushed from meeting to meeting. She headed over to Seven on her lunch hour entering through the waiting room—a no-no, but given that she was irritated and in a hurry, she didn't care. She noted that it was full of men, most of them in suits. *How ironic that when the rest of the world was eating lunch . . .*

Addison sat down at Sondra's desk and removed her salad from her bag. She picked up the file with Mr. X written across the top directly above a CLASSIFIED stamp. *Mr. X, huh.* She opened it, curiously flipping through when her phone rang. Addison picked up. It was her assistant informing her that she had a meeting pop up. It was an appointment they'd desperately been trying to get. *She had to take it.* And, of course, it started in forty-five minutes across town. *Shit.* Addison stared at the file. She flipped straight to the back and quickly read over Mr. X's preferences. He was seeking corporal punishment using whips but mostly preferred the use of hands combined with choking and was to be told he was worthless and would never amount to anything. A certain musical selection must be on repeat throughout the session. Mr. X's sole focus was on the B&D aspect of BDSM. He wanted bondage and discipline. So long as no marks were left above the neck. *Perfect. He was pretty typical, but clean, easy, and very psychical in terms of client needs. Almost clinical.*

Addison read a bit further and then peeked at the time. She had to go. She gathered her things and left the file lying on the desk. Glancing back, she told herself she knew all she needed to know. *Beat the shit out of him while wearing a mask and they were good.*

~

LATER THAT EVENING, Addison arrived back at Seven to find the outfit that was left for her. Black high-waisted slacks with cute buttons down the front, a crisp, short sleeve white button-down shirt, both with tags on them. Lying next to the clothes was a pair of shiny black peep toe Christian Louboutin pumps. *Huh.* Despite the fact that she resembled a waitress, this ensemble could've come from her own closet. She didn't recall reading about this in the client profile but it was different from her other clients, who preferred latex and leather. Attached to the shoes was a note. *Put your hair in a bun. And put the mask on, all the way.* She held the mask up to her face. It went all the way around her head. *Strange.*

Suddenly, her phone rang, startling her. She removed the mask, and listened as, once again, Sondra ran through the rules. She must have said the same thing six times at the very least. *Don't break character. Stick to the routine. Don't speak to him. No matter what— don't speak. Press play on the iPad in the corner. The music is to play on repeat the entire session.*

"It's important. You've said that..."

Sondra cleared her throat. "It's more than important. This session is dangerous, Addison. You must promise me that you'll follow my instructions down to the letter."

She grimaced. "Dangerous? How? Am I in physical danger?"

"I don't think so. But let's just say this one is tough to break ... mentally. So, keep your guard up, ok?"

Addison studied herself in the mirror. She looked healthy —thin, yet strong. Andre was changing her body for the better. "Ok. I got it. DON'T MESS THIS UP."

Sondra sighed, sounding exasperated. "Just promise me you'll keep your head in the game and stay smart."

Addison slipped the mask on. *It was hard to breathe in this damn thing.*

"Promise," she replied, though it was muffled.

ADDISON FROZE dead in her tracks as she opened the door to the dimly lit room and stepped inside. She gasped audibly, her throat tightened and her mouth went dry. William looked up as a confused expression crossed his face. Then she realized, she had the mask on. He couldn't see her face. Suddenly, Sondra's words echoed in her mind. *Keep it together no matter what.*

Addison walked over to the iPad in the corner and glanced at the display. Pettersson's Symphony No. Seven was set on repeat. Pressing play, she slowly walked over toward William, who was sitting in a chair in the center of the room. Standing in front of him, she placed the collar around his neck, a little tighter than she probably should have. He kept his gaze glued to the floor.

Addison stepped back, taking him in. The sight of him made her tear up. *Keep your head in the game.* He was beautiful, like a work of art, the way he sat in the chair with his chiseled body. But he was different, broken, his face twisted. Pained. She'd seen that look enough times now to know a broken man when she saw one. How was it possible that the man before her was the same William she knew? So many emotions ran through her mind. *What in the hell was he doing here? And why had Sondra put her in this position?*

Suddenly, Addison became enraged. *Don't break character.* She'd had it with Sondra, with William, with Patrick, with everyone and she intended to use it. Her emotions spilled out. Anger poured out of her. The blow that struck William across the face hit him with such force that spit flew from his mouth. The blow caused her hand to throb but she barely felt the pain. She was numb.

Addison took hold of the hair on his head and lifted his face to her. She struck him again and again. When all the breath had gone out of her, she let go of his hair. William let his head fall as tears seeped from the corners of his eyes.

"Enough?" she asked, her voice low and raw.

He shook his head.

Addison slapped him. Once at first, and then several times more. He hung his head. She gave it everything she had, allowing the feelings she'd pent up inside over the last few months, maybe her whole life, come to the surface, fueling her rage.

When she'd had enough, depleted and panting, she turned and walked to the desk in the back of the room. Tears stung her cheeks, staining the inside of her mask as she took out a note card and scribbled her message. *You're not even worth a full session. You're not worth anything, much less my time. Get out.*

Walking over to William, she carefully removed the collar. Bending at the knee, Addison studied his face. Unable to help herself, she kissed his cheek where it was still wet with the tears that had fallen. William flinched and visibly recoiled. The mask hadn't allowed her skin to touch his. Needing to feel him, she trailed her fingers down his face, the lines already etched in her memory. Then she placed the note in his hand, curled his fingers around it, and turned and left the room.

Back in Sondra's office, she flung the mask, collapsed onto the couch and sobbed until there was nothing left. Addison stayed there for a long while as her mind ran back and forth over all of the ways she should have seen this coming. She should have known it would only be a matter of time before she'd end up broken, too.

Finally, when there were no more tears left to cry, she pulled herself together. She gathered her things, went to Sondra's desk, picked up the file and stuffed it in her bag. *CLASSIFIED, my ass.*

ADDISON COULDN'T GET HOME FAST ENOUGH. She needed to hold her boys—to tell them how much she loved them, how much she wanted them, and how proud she was. She knew she was a good mother, and yet she still wondered if it was enough—*if she was enough*. Did she tell them she loved them often enough? Were they going to end up like her clients? Like her? Feeling unlovable and unworthy, never quite good enough, remedying their pain by attaching themselves to all the wrong things, anything to fill the void.

She wouldn't let that happen. She couldn't let that happen.

Her phone lit up. Again. Sondra had called at least five dozen times since she'd left Seven. *Fuck Sondra.*

Once home, she relieved Kelsey, telling her to go home. Addison needed to be alone.

Later, after she'd showered, she tiptoed into Connor's room and sat on the edge of his bed. Addison watched the rise and fall of his chest as he slept and inhaled his little boy scent. He was growing up so fast and yet, more often than not, he was still trapped somewhere between a little kid and a big kid. Some days he tried on the big kid outfit for size. While others, he seemed content to wear the little kid uniform. He wore them equally well, although, neither quite fit, one still too big, the other too small. Addison stayed, watching him sleep. She studied his face and breathed in his innocence. He smiled in his sleep. Silent tears fell as she thought of William, of what she'd done to him and why. She cried, remembering the times she'd cried herself to sleep at his age because no one had cared enough to comfort her. She cried for the little girl she was back then and for what a shame it was that no one had ever loved her this much.

ADDISON AWOKE LATER in the darkness, shaking. She must've fallen asleep in Connor's bed. Her muscles ached, her body was stiff. *You're ok, she told herself. It was just a bad dream.* She sat up, trying to shake it off. In the dream, she was naked, chained, and locked in a cage. Her body was battered and bruised. *It was just a nightmare, she told herself again.* Rattled and wide-awake, she forced herself to go downstairs and put on hot tea. Still shaken, she waited for the tea to boil and then took it into the living room where she removed

William's client folder from her bag, curled up on the couch, and began reading.

Due to the nature of work and celebrity in which this client is involved, the client will be referred to only as Mr. X in all correspondence.

Over the course of seven years, from five to twelve years of age, Mr. X was brutally tortured and abused daily at the hands of his stepfather. The abuse was ritualistic in nature, taking place each day as his stepfather arrived home from the office. Mr. X was expected to be waiting at the door holding a scotch, made to perfection, just the way his stepfather liked it: chilled with two ice cubes. The scotch had to reach a certain level on the glass. No more, no less. After his stepfather tossed his drink back, he instructed Mr. X to put on Pettersson's Symphony No. Seven and remove his clothes. Once undressed he'd beat him for the duration of the piece. When the music ended, although sometimes he ordered that it be played again, his stepfather would tell Mr. X that "he knew the little bastard was just using him for money, mooching off of him" and that "he was so worthless his own father didn't even want him." He instructed Mr. X to repeat the same sentence seven times over: He would never be as successful as his stepfather was because he was a worthless piece of shit.

Over time, Mr. X learned not to show any emotion during the beatings. Otherwise, the intensity was far more severe and lasted longer in duration. When asked where his mother was, Mr. X replied only that it was the time of her daily massage. When questioned whether or not she knew about the beatings he endured at the hands of his stepfather, Mr. X commented that he wasn't sure, but that he thought she had suspected.

At the age of eleven, his mother divorced the abuser and remarried.

Mr. X has implied that with the new stepfather there was a short reprieve and that eventually the abuse continued, though the physical beatings were less intense while the verbal assaults held the same, if not increased, intensity.

Mr. X has made significant progress during his time as my client. In the beginning, he was unable to show any sign of emotion and had a difficult time performing as a submissive. Although over time he has shown improvement, his capability to feel and/or exhibit emotion still remains severely limited.

It is my personal opinion that Mr. X suffers from Reactive Attachment Disorder (RAD) marked by emotional detachment in the second sense: a decision to avoid engaging emotional connections, rather than an inability or difficulty in doing so, typically for personal, social, or other reasons. In this sense, it allows him to maintain boundaries, psychic integrity, and avoid undesired impact by or upon others, related to emotional demands. As such, it is a deliberate mental attitude, which avoids engaging the emotions of others.

Addison set the file down, unable to read any further. She forced herself to breathe. Her mind wandered to William and memories of the time they'd spent together. Suddenly, there was clarity where there had been none. There were little things that, at the time, she had thought were odd which now made perfect sense.

Reading his profile exhausted her, physically and emotionally. William, who had never been able to emotionally connect with anyone, had fallen in love with her. And the realization that she'd hurt him utilizing the very tactics he was trying to overcome was more than she could handle. She'd lied to him in an attempt to keep from getting hurt herself. But she hadn't really seen what she was doing as being hurtful to him. She was simply playing his game. Given his playboy reputation, she figured that he wasn't the type who wanted anything more than casual sex. And she was ok with that. What she hadn't considered was that his reputation had more to do with the fact that he *couldn't* give more, not that he hadn't wanted to. She could see clearly now why he was attracted to her: she'd never demanded anything from him on an emotional level, which was easy because she was married.

It made sense why their connection was so intense, why they couldn't seem to stay away from one another. She and William were one and the same: both broken, both confined by their past, both adding fuel to the other's flames. But Addison was smart enough to know what happened when you played with fire. You got burned.

CHAPTER SEVENTEEN

The following morning, Addison had originally planned on calling in sick. For one, she hadn't slept. Two, she was emotionally and physically spent. It wasn't until Andre showed up and coached her through one of his signature grueling workouts that she surprisingly found her second wind and decided that it wouldn't hurt her to go into the office for a little while. She needed to have a few words with Sondra, anyway.

She showered and dressed in a long t-shirt dress and sandals; she was going casual today. Her days of caring what Sondra thought, or anyone else for that matter, were over.

Once downstairs, she sat sipping her coffee and watched the boys enjoying their breakfast carefully prepared by the chef that her lies were paying for. She listened to their laughter and wondered how anything could be more perfect. *This is what matters.* Addison realized she needed to spend more time at home. She didn't have any work scheduled at Seven this weekend. Maybe they'd get away, just the three of them.

Addison heard her driver pull up, and as she kissed and

hugged the boys, she lingered. "You know how much I love you guys, right?"

"Yes, Mama," the boys replied in unison.

She laughed and threw open her arms, extending them as wide as she could. "THIS much!"

Parker climbed down from his chair and ran to her, hugging her knee. "I wuv you this much, Mama."

Addison's heart slowly melted into a million tiny pieces. Being a mother was hard, painfully hard sometimes, but moments like these were what made it all worth it. She bent down and wrapped Parker in the biggest bear hug she could muster, considering how sore she was, until he begged for mercy. Before long, the other boys joined in, and the four of them piled on top of one another, tickling each other and laughing like lunatics on the kitchen floor. At the time, she had no idea it would be this lasting memory that would hold her together over the next forty-eight hours. She didn't know she would conjure up thoughts of this very moment as she begged for her life and tried to survive the most horrific, excruciating situation one could possibly imagine. If she had, she would have stayed a little longer.

NOT SURPRISINGLY, Sondra was waiting in Addison's office when she arrived. Addison set her things down, walked to her desk, and sat down without saying a word, pretending she wasn't there.

Sondra eyed her up and down, blatantly displeased. "What in the hell are you wearing?"

She shrugged her shoulders. "Whatever I damn well please," she said. She hadn't realized she was as angry as she was, not until the words slipped out.

Sondra tried another direction. "You aren't taking my calls…" she hissed. "Are you trying to break contract?"

Addison held her phone to her face, scanning her emails. "I've been busy," she said glancing up. "But then, *you* of all people should know that."

"Look, Addison, I understand I put you in a difficult position. But in this line of work one has to be capable of handling her emotions and putting them aside when the situation calls for it."

"And?"

Sondra furrowed her brow. "And . . . act like an adult about it."

Addison placed her phone on the desk and looked Sondra dead in the eye. "Look— I completed the session. I did what you wanted. I followed *your* rules. So, I'm not sure why you're here."

Sondra folded her arms and thought carefully about what to say next. "I'm here because you refused to take my calls. And, because I have something important, *something big* to tell you… You were fantastic, Addison. You pulled it off. He wants to see you again. Tonight."

Addison's eyes grew wide. Her jaw tightened. She was *this* close to losing her shit. "Fuck you, Sondra," she said, before cocking her head to the side. "I agreed to six clients. Not seven. So, tell me, are YOU trying to break contract? Because I dare you. Hell, at this point, I *beg* you," she added with a shrug. "Go ahead—try me."

Sondra shook her head. "Addison, he asked to see you from here on out. He told me he felt a connection that he'd never felt before. This is HUGE!"

Addison stared.

"Don't you have anything to say? Aren't there any questions you want to ask?"

"No." Addison told her. Then she stood, anger building

insider her, begging to be unleashed. Maybe it was the relentless training, or maybe it was the fact that she knew she had been played, but she saw it for what it was. Red, hot, rage. She walked around the desk to where Sondra sat. "Well, actually, there is. How could you?" she asked, sticking her finger in Sondra's face, forcing her backward. "I have bent over backward for you . . . for this agency. And you throw me under the bus? Just like that?" Addison took a step back afraid she might do something she would regret. She placed her hands on her hips, dropped them, and then balled her fists. "You could've told me. You could've warned me! Months ago! You know—said something along the lines of stay away from that one. He's trouble. You'll fall in love. Only he won't love you back. BECAUSE HE CAN'T!"

She waited for Sondra to say something but when she didn't she realized it was because she was backed into a corner. She studied Sondra's expression, disgust playing across her face.

Meanwhile, a smile played at Sondra's lips. Addison realized she wasn't worth it. Clearly, she enjoyed the sick games she played. *Never break character.* Sondra shifted. "I didn't need to warn you, Addison. You weren't the one I was worried about, because you're stronger than you think. And you were seeing my star client. You were helping him. That's *why* I chose you for Seven. You have the ability to connect with people on a level I've never seen. You draw them in and hold them captive."

"I don't want to hold anyone captive. What I want is honesty. Integrity…"

Sondra's brow rose. "You helped William on both a personal level and as his Mistress. Sure, I know I fucked up by not telling you beforehand, but I needed you to understand. And I knew you wouldn't—not unless you saw for yourself."

Addison narrowed her gaze. "What is there to understand?"

Sondra sighed, wondering whether she should tell her the truth. In the end, Addison had asked for honesty and Sondra figured it was *now or never*. "Fifteen years ago, William Hartman became my first client. It didn't start out that way. We were . . . together . . . *sexually*."

Addison inhaled deeply and let it out cutting Sondra off. "Why does that not surprise me?"

"Wait—let me finish—" Sondra started and then paused to make sure Addison was ready. "He was different then, Addison. A different man than the William you know. He was strictly dominant. He wouldn't even allow me to touch him . . . not during the act. And not afterward. He couldn't make eye contact or speak so long as he was undressed. He was rough, abusive even. And I had been dominant my whole life, so, as you can imagine, the two didn't go over too well. Things were . . . let's just say. . . pretty intense—"

Addison held her palm up. "I don't want to hear this."

"Maybe not. But you need to."

Addison rubbed at the back of her neck, essentially giving Sondra permission to continue. "At the time, I had just started to get into BDSM. Anyway— to make a long story short— you could say that I made it my personal mission to 'turn' him. The surprising thing was that my forcing him to submit opened him up. He enjoyed it and eventually it helped him talk about what had happened to him as a child. We knew there was no *real* relationship there. It was about sex and about something we both needed at the time. At some point, we decided that since I'd helped him, maybe I could help others. And that's how Seven was born. William became the financial backer and part owner. But if he knew —if he had any inkling at all that you were involved—well, it would be the end of it. Probably the end of me, too. He loves you, Addison. He told me as much. William doesn't talk about emotions. Not lightly. I know the way I handled things wasn't fair to either of you. But you needed to know. You needed to see the truth. And, in a way, so did he. You see, the truth is… it is possible for people like William to love, but it's *because* of Seven. It's because of the work that we do there."

Addison felt sick. "What is it that you're asking me, Sondra? Because I'm not going to keep lying to him."

"I understand. But what I'm saying is that if you're going to cut William out of your personal life, then fine. But don't cut him out as your submissive. He's too weak right now. He has come so far but he's still very fragile. William is a dear friend. And I care about him."

Addison was furious, but also, devastated. The worst part was that she wasn't sure whether it had to do with what Sondra was asking her or whether it was picturing the two of them together that bothered her the most.

She stood, walked to the door, and opened it. "I have nothing left to say. Please leave."

Sondra didn't budge. "I understand that you're upset. And this is probably a lot for you to take in. But, please do consider what I've said. Just take some time and let it sink in, ok?"

Addison didn't need time. She already knew what she had to do. She motioned Sondra towards the door with a wry smile. "Tell Mr. Hartman his Mistress will see him this evening."

Sondra looked stunned. "So, we agree, then? Are you sure, Addison?" she asked, pursing her lips. "I need you to be sure because you cannot mess this up. It'll only set him back in his treatment."

Addison looked her straight in the eye. "I've never been more certain in my life."

~

Knowing she had a lot to do between now and the time she saw William later that evening, Addison hurried from one interview to the next. She was anxious but excited, too. Having finally made a decision about the direction her life was taking, she felt good about moving forward.

With a few minutes to spare before her last interview of the day, she dialed Patrick's cell phone. When he didn't pick up, she left a message explaining that she was taking the boys to the beach for a few days, specifically that they were leaving that evening, and that she would call him when they got back. The last thing she wanted was for him to fly home once he'd received the paperwork: the paperwork that would legally separate the two of them. She hadn't yet decided whether or not she'd file for divorce, but filing for legal separation wouldn't hurt, given the fact that he was already halfway across the world. If Patrick didn't want to be a husband or a father, it was high time he admitted it. It wasn't that she didn't love him, she did. That was the point. She was giving him an out.

Thankfully, understanding why Addison needed to get away, Jessica had been more than happy to loan Addison her family's beach house. *God, she was so grateful for Jessica, especially these past few weeks.* Jess had always been an amazingly loyal friend. It helped that she could tell her anything and Jessica would listen, usually offering advice that made her laugh. And while Jessica threatened to write it all down, swearing that it made great material for her first bestseller, Addison knew that when it came right down to it, her secrets were safe. Because if nothing else, Jessica promised she would at least give Addison the courtesy of changing her name.

ADDISON HAD to make a few stops for supplies before heading to her final interview of the day. It was located on a rural route, and even though she'd checked her map and the directions several times, she couldn't find the location of the estate. Not knowing the area, she quickly found herself lost. She pulled up Google Maps on her phone, but being out in the middle of nowhere, her internet wasn't loading. Frustrated that she was going to be late, she called her assistant. When her assistant failed to pick up, Addison left her a message explaining that she was lost, gave her the address she needed to find, and asked her to call her back ASAP. Finally, out of options and running late, she called her potential client and explained that she was lost. And although she was embarrassed, Addison was incredibly grateful when the man insisted on coming to get her, allowing her to follow him back to the estate.

She checked her appearance in the rearview mirror and suddenly regretted having dressed so casually. She was reapplying her lipstick as the black truck pulled up beside her. She smiled at the driver and he smiled back. That's when she noticed the man in the driver seat looked familiar. She was almost certain she'd met him before. She watched as he got out of the car and walked toward her. As she rolled down her window, she racked her brain trying to put a name to his face. The man extended his hand. It was as Addison reached out to shake it that she noticed the look in his eye and the hair on the back of her neck stood on end. She attempted to recoil her hand, but her attempt was a few seconds too late. She felt the jab as something cold and sharp pierced her skin. Unfortunately, that would be the last conscious thought Addison would have over the next forty-eight hours.

SCOTT HAMMONS WAS PLEASED with the work he'd done and knew God was pleased, too. He eyed Addison Greyer, naked and unconscious in the room he'd set up for the occasion. He'd given her enough Ketamine to keep her out for at least the next twelve hours or so. He walked over, checked her pulse, and injected a little Rohypnol for good measure. When she finally awoke, she would be dazed and confused, with little memory of how she'd gotten here. Everything was going to be perfect.

It had to be perfect. He had put a lot of energy into seeing that everything went according to plan. First, he'd rented this hellhole of a place: a small old farmhouse, remotely located, just off a rural road. Out in the middle of nowhere, it was the type of place where no one would hear her screams or bother him while he carried out God's work. He'd visited various hardware stores to buy the supplies he would need, mindful not to shop in just one place, always careful not to raise suspicion. He concocted the plan to secure an interview with Mrs. Greyer, even making up a fictitious name and address because he was a smart man. That's what smart men did. They prepared and they were patient. That is why God spoke to him. That is why God chose him in the first place.

Over the next forty-eight hours, he would get his revenge for all of the ways William Hartman had wronged him: for taking away his business, for dismantling his life. First, he would bind, beat, and torture the love of Hartman's life. Because the Bible said: *"'There is no peace,' says the Lord, 'for the wicked.'"* And William Hartman shall have no peace.

Next, he would call William Hartman from a disposable cell phone, of course. He was a smart man after all, no matter what anyone said, especially evildoers like Hartman. He'd give him the fictitious name and tell him that he was holding

Mrs. Greyer captive. Hartman would believe him because, by now, someone would've noticed that the stupid bitch was missing. He would even use the disposable phone to text him a picture of his whore, chained and bloodied.

Then he would order Hartman to meet him, alone, and because Scott was a smart and capable man, he would watch and wait, stalking his prey until he was certain that he'd arrived alone. Given his genius, he would then send him to a second location, just because he could. It would be the third location where Scott would finally show himself, *the third time's the charm,* and where he would revel in the delight of Hartman's bewilderment—his astonishment at the brilliant man who'd just deceived him. Since Scott was doing God's work, by removing the evildoers from this world, he would instruct Hartman to handcuff himself, and then he'd drug him just as he had his whore. The Bible said: *"He who commits adultery lacks sense; he who does it destroys himself."* Hartman had committed adultery and because Scott knew he was an angel of the Lord, he understood that he had to carry out God's work. He also knew that Hartman would be forced to comply if he wanted to save the woman he loved. After all, the Bible said, *"And ye shall know the truth, and the truth shall make you free."* Scott knew the truth because God had told him as much and the truth was that William had to die.

CHAPTER EIGHTEEN

"What do you mean she didn't show?" Sondra asked exasperated.

"Just what I said. I waited an hour. And she didn't show," William replied matter of factly.

Sondra sighed. "All right. Let me figure out what's going on... I'll call you back."

Goddammit, Addison. She was going to kill that girl. She should've known. Sondra dialed her number. It went straight to voice mail. *Big surprise.* Next, she tried Addison's home number. A girl picked up. "She's not home. May I ask who is calling?"

"This is her boss. It's very important that I speak with her immediately. When she gets in, can you make sure she calls me right away?"

"Yes," the girl said and then paused. "Well, actually, I was going to call the office. She's supposed to be here to take the kids. I had class two hours ago, and I missed it because she didn't show," she told Sondra with a sigh. "It's not like her, and I'm kind of worried."

Sondra rubbed her temples. *Great,* this is exactly what she needed. "Well, why are you telling me?"

"Because you're her boss. I thought you might know where she was..."

"If I knew where she was, I wouldn't be calling, WOULD I?" Sondra said before she slammed the phone down. *God, she should've known Addison couldn't handle this. Why'd she have to go and tell her the truth?*

Sondra thought for a moment, finally dialing Addison's assistant. She explained that she hadn't seen Addison but that she'd received a message from her that she was lost en route to an interview and that when she tried to call her back her phone just went to voice mail. Sondra wrote down the client's name and phone number. *Damn it. If she messed this up, too . . .*

She dialed the phone number the assistant had given her. The number was disconnected.

Annoyed, Sondra figured Addison would come around sooner or later and decided to let it go, until, a few hours later when her phone rang. It was Addison's home number that showed up on the screen, only it wasn't Addison. It was the nanny calling.

"Hello?"

"Um...I'm worried about Mrs. Greyer."

Sondra checked the time. "You haven't heard from her?"

"No. And she was supposed to take the boys to the beach this weekend. She asked me to have them packed, saying that they were going to leave at seven when she got home. They've been waiting impatiently for hours..." she said and then she exhaled slowly. "It's not like her to tell them something and then not follow through. It's especially not like her not to come home when she says. I'm thinking about calling the police... What do you think?"

Sondra sat up in bed. "No— Don't do that. Let me make a

few calls… I'm sure it's just a misunderstanding. I'll locate her. Are you ok there with the children or shall I send someone else?"

"They're pretty upset, so I'll stay with them."

Sondra rubbed at her chin. "All right, call me if she turns up at home."

Sondra hung up the phone and dialed Addison's assistant, who answered on the first ring. "The client that Mrs. Greyer went to interview, get me that address. In fact, send me all of the information you have. Immediately."

"Certainly. I'll send it right over. Is everything ok?"

Sondra swallowed hard. "I sure hope so," she told her and ended the call.

Next, Sondra rang Liselle, who confirmed what she already knew—that Addison hadn't ever shown up at Seven.

Her inbox chimed. Sondra opened the email containing the client's information. Simon Peter: 555-452-9111. It was the same number she'd called before. Sondra dialed the number again. Still disconnected. She tried Addison's cell, which went straight to voice mail, again. Sondra typed the name and address into the agency system, which turned up nothing. Then she tried Google, which also turned up nothing.

Sondra called Addison's assistant back. "Did you run background checks on Mr. Simon Peter?"

"No," the girl told her. "I thought Mrs. Greyer had."

Sondra slammed her fist down. "Goddammit. I need you to check the system on your end. Mine isn't showing. See if anything has been run. NOW!"

The girl did as she was told and came back on the line a few moments later. "There is no one in the system by that name. A check wasn't run on Simon Peter. Should I check another name?"

"Fuck," Sondra repeated. She swallowed hard and hung up the phone.

She was hesitant to call William Hartman, but what else could she do? It was him or the police, and, until she knew for sure that something bad happened, she preferred to leave the cops out of this.

Sondra needed help and William was one of her few friends. Since he had unlimited resources at his disposal, in addition to the fact that he was in love with Addison, she knew she had no choice but to involve him in the matter, even if it meant extreme repercussions for herself. She threw a few things in a bag and texted William that she needed to see him and was on her way over.

William was waiting for her at the door, wearing plaid pajama bottoms that were slung low on his hips and nothing else. Even after all this time, seeing him this way still made something in her shift. She felt it deep down, a familiarity, but nothing more.

It didn't help that he grinned wickedly. "So, I take it you're here to do my session? Why *here*?" he asked and then he cocked his head. "What happened to *Laelia*, anyway?"

"William…"

He paused and looked out the window, a smile playing across his lips as though he hadn't heard her at all. "Damn, I really, *really* liked that girl," he said and she realized he hadn't.

Sondra froze. Seeing the look on his face, she lost every ounce of courage she might've had and decided right then and there that explaining everything was a bad idea. "She's, uh, tied up."

William laughed. "Nice pun. I'd like to tie her up."

Sondra took a seat at the bar. "I need water. Do you have a Perrier?"

William walked over, opened the fridge, took out the bottle, opened it, and slid it across the bar to Sondra.

"So, what's up?" he asked, nodding, suddenly looking weary.

Sondra gulped the water. *Here goes nothing.* "I'm here about Addison Greyer. She's missing."

His eyes shifted. "What do you mean she's missing? What the fuc—?"

Sondra cut him off. "Sit down, William."

William stayed put.

Sondra held her hands up to silence him. "Listen, she went to interview a potential client this afternoon, and no one has heard from her since. The nanny said she didn't show up to get the kids. And when I typed the client's name into our database, nothing came up. I Googled his name and address. It doesn't exist."

William's expression changed from wary to stone cold. He picked up his phone from the bar and began dialing numbers. "What time was this? How long has she been missing?" he demanded. Sondra knew what he was doing. He was analyzing the risk, he knew the statistics.

She pressed her lips together. "Six hours. Who are you calling?"

"Addison. I'm calling Addison!" William paced back and forth. *Come on. Pick up.* Nothing. It went straight to voicemail. Next, he dialed Carl. "Assemble the team. I need everyone in here ASAP."

William kept pacing and firing questions. "How did this happen? Has anyone notified the police? Her husband? Checked with the rest of her family?"

"No," Sondra said, trying to remain calm for William's sake.

"She wouldn't just not come home to her children or ignore Kelsey's calls. Something bad has happened to her,

Sondra," he assured her. "Why in the hell didn't you call me sooner? Or call the fucking police?"

"I wasn't sure she was really missing. I mean . . . This isn't the first time my calls have gone unanswered."

Thankfully, William's security team came through the door at that moment, taking the attention and the pressure off of her. She listened as William explained everything to them, and then Carl interrogated Sondra, asking her the same questions multiple times, until he seemed satisfied with her answers. She forwarded the email with the client information.

There was something about the way Carl looked at her when she'd given him the client's name. She noticed his expression was off when he pulled up the email. There was something behind that look that terrified her. All at once, the room was in motion; there were calls being made and computers being set up. Not knowing what to do with herself, Sondra went to Carl and tapped him on the shoulder, interrupting his conversation. "Do you know someone by the name of Simon Peter?"

Carl looked at Sondra, though his expression gave nothing away. "Why do you ask?"

Sondra crossed her arms, feeling uneasy. "I just need to know."

Carl nodded. "Simon Peter was one of the twelve apostles of Jesus. The leader—he was known for bringing people to Jesus."

Sondra didn't follow. "Ok?"

Carl spoke slowly, carefully choosing his words. "The name this person, this client, choose to give, gives us a glimpse into his mental state. We've been dealing with someone like this for the past few months, he keeps sending letters."

Sondra tilted her head. "Couldn't it just be a coincidence?"

She watched as his bottom lip jutted out. "It's possible," he said. "Just highly unlikely."

~

ADDISON HEARD the sounds of doors opening. She opened her eyes as best she could. She saw the man walk towards her, noticing him holding something. Reflexively, she flinched.

"Steady now," the man said.

She tried to move, to gain some leeway, wiggling just a little. She felt the jab and then the sting where the needle had gone into her arm. She tried to jerk away but couldn't. Everything was so hazy. She was so tired.

When the man spoke, he was so close she felt his breath on her ear. "I told you, if you keep moving like that I'm going to have to keep doing this. You're a hardheaded little bitch, aren't you?"

It took all the strength she had, but she managed to shake her head. *He's drugging you. Pull it together. You know this man. You know this voice. Think Addison. Think.*

The man laughed. "Rest well, little whore," he said, patting the top of her head. "Rest well. You're going to need it…"

Addison listened as he closed the door to the cage. She heard the rattling of keys and then his feet climb the stairs. Next, the room went pitch black. In a matter of seconds, she was out cold again.

~

WILLIAM'S TEAM was able to track down Addison's cellphone

within a few hours. From there, they were able to locate her car, which they found abandoned, with her purse still inside. At that point, it became clear, it was inevitable that they needed to get the police involved. William and Sondra met with the police together and then the FBI, each of them giving limited details regarding their respective relationships with Addison Greyer. William explained that he was a friend trying to help Sondra. He understood that if he disclosed the nature of their relationship at that point, it would do Addison no favors. They'd laser focus their attention on him. *Better to let them figure it out on their own. But in the meantime, at least they'd be looking.*

As for Sondra, to the cops she was simply just Addison Greyer's boss. There was no need to indulge any further. She realized she'd be forced to hand over her list of clients and she wasn't ready to do that, not yet. After all, all signs pointed to this having to do with Addison's work at the agency, not at *Seven*. Still, William and Sondra weren't stupid. They both knew it was only a matter of time before the truth would come out. Fortunately for them, and for Addison, the longer that was avoided, the better. Because once the truth was out, it would mark a noticeable shift in the investigation. The truth would turn the investigation inward, when the authorities would stop looking for the person who really held Addison Greyer captive, and instead focus solely on those who were lying. Unfortunately for Addison, this shift would likely prove fatal.

The police contacted Patrick, who chartered a flight home. William reached out to all of the major media outlets and pulled strings, getting Addison's picture out and scoring Sondra interviews on the next day's morning shows. All of a sudden, there was a flurry of activity, and the situation became overwhelmingly intense. It was clearly evident that, due to the circumstances surrounding Addison's disappearance, all parties understood that time was of the essence.

CHAPTER NINETEEN

Addison awoke to liquid being forced down her throat. She was choking, drowning. Through the ringing in her ears, she heard the sound of a camera. It was snapping photos. *Click. Click. Click.*

"Wake up," the voice said, as he slapped her over and over. "Your sleeping is fucking this up."

She felt the vomit rise in her throat. Addison forced her eyes open. Then she felt the cold. He was hosing her down and the water was frigid. The man was standing above her, an angry expression on his face. She sat up as best she could.

"You stupid bitch. You had me worried... I thought you ruined everything," the man repeated over and over as he sprayed her.

Addison sensed déjà vu. She had been in this situation before. *She had woken like this before.* Observing her surroundings, she took everything in. Badly beaten and bleeding, she tasted a mixture of blood and something else . . . vomit. Her hands and feet were shackled, and she was in a small cage, maybe five by five feet. They looked to be in a basement of some sort. It was smelly, dark, and cold, so it had to be underground.

"Good. You're coming around. The drugs are finally wearing off..." the man told her, dropping the hose. Addison stared at him. *She knew him.* He was the man on the boat—the man from Capri.

She chose her words carefully. "Mr. Hammons?"

He laughed an evil laugh. "That would be me."

Addison cocked her head to the side and waited for him to say more.

He didn't. He simply walked to a table set up in the corner. He grabbed a plate and walked toward Addison, placing a sandwich in her hand. "I bet you're wondering what you're doing here..."

She took small, careful bites, trying to wash away the bitter taste of her own blood. As she did, she eyed Scott Hammons, analyzing him. She thought back on the times she'd woken up before. *How many was it now? Three or four?* She recalled the first time, or what she thought had been the first time, the time she was beaten and suspended. Then there was the time he masturbated in front of her and now this. Although, she had no idea how long she'd been out, Addison assumed that it had been long enough that people were beginning to look for her. Her thoughts went to the boys as she imagined their faces and her hugging them in the kitchen.

Addison swallowed a small bite. "I am wondering, yes."

Scott closed the cage door and locked it. He drug the chair across the room and then he sat and folded his arms, watching her as he sipped what smelled like whiskey. Addison wasn't sure he was going to answer her, until finally he spoke. "You're William Hartman's whore. That's what you're doing here. He owes me..." he said, taking a gulp of his drink. "And I guess you could say, I'm collecting on what's due."

Addison sat up straighter. *Keep him talking.* "I don't understand."

"Your lover boy, he stole from me. It's his turn to pay up. That's why you're here."

Listen. And buy time. He is going to kill you. Addison thought for a moment, considering how she'd respond. With sudden clarity, she devised a plan, her Domme training kicking in full gear. She laughed louder than the situation probably called for. "You think I'm William's whore?" she asked and then she laughed again. It hurt. "That's funny."

His face went pale. Clearly, Scott Hammons was taken aback. He eyed Addison up and down and kicked back his whiskey. "Don't fuck with me."

She pursed her lips. "I'm not William's whore. I'm his Dominatrix. And the bastard owes me a lot of money. So, I highly doubt he gives a shit whether I live or die."

"His what?"

"His Dominatrix. He pays me to beat the shit out of him."

Scott chuckled. "And why would he do that?"

"Because he's crazy. Because he steals and cheats people. People like you. And, apparently, people like me. And then, just so he doesn't feel too badly about it, he enjoys getting slapped around to ease his conscience."

Scott stood and poured himself another whiskey. "I saw the way he looked at you. He's in love with you. I've sent him your photos—photos of you—like this. I'm sure I'll be hearing from him soon."

She didn't skip a beat. "Perhaps."

"Perhaps what?" he asked, confused.

"Perhaps he'll come," she said and she shrugged. She winced. The pain was unbearable, but she knew better than to let it show. "Perhaps he won't," she added, matter of factly.

Scott's face reddened. He stood, throwing his glass against the wall, watching as it shattered into a million pieces. "What do you mean *perhaps*?"

Addison thought quickly. "Well, for one, I'm blackmailing him, so if he shows up, it'll only be so that he can kill me himself."

Scott stumbled to the corner of the room, clearly drunk. He walked towards the crank he used to suspend her in the air. Addison remembered waking up suspended before. He cranked the lever and slowly she rose until she hovered off the ground. Walking furiously toward the cage, he grabbed the belt from the table. She squeezed her eyes shut. *He was angry.* And he was going to take it out on her, *which meant he was buying it.* Scott struggled with the lock. She remained quiet, unwilling to give him satisfaction and not wanting to further incite his anger. He continued struggling with the lock, which only infuriated him more, until finally he managed to open it. Once inside, he raised the belt, striking her across the backside with as much force as he could muster. Addison held her breath. He walked around the front, striking her again. Smelling the mixture of blood and whiskey, she felt herself fading, but did her best to focus on her senses. He hit her twice more and then he seemed spent. "I know what you're up to," he slurred. "You're trying to trick me."

Addison stared him straight in the eye and called his bluff. "If you're going to kill me— do it now. Because I'd rather you go ahead and get it over with rather than give William Hartman the satisfaction, *if and when*, he shows up." Scott stared at the ground, concentrating hard. "It's clear that you have a lot of anger towards William Hartman. I don't blame you. I hate the bastard, too, which is why I'm black-mailing him. What I want to know is, what he did to you that made you hate him so much. Because I can't imagine it's worse than what he's done to me," she added.

Rapport building. That's what this was called. Addison said a silent thank you for her training as Domme; she had never guessed in a million years that it might one day help save her own life. "I mean… if you'd like, I can tell you what he did to me. Thing is, it's a thousand times worse than any beating you could give me. Hell, you could do this all day long and it wouldn't touch what he's done."

She studied his face. His expression was blank, his eyes dark and empty. But for the first time she could swear she saw a subtle hint of emotion, somewhere down deep, locked inside. He closed the cage, though he didn't replace the lock, and took his seat in the chair. Picking up the whiskey, he drank straight from the bottle. "William Hartman stole my life. He took everything: my family, my business . . . everything. And the Bible says: *'Thou shall not steal.'* William stole. And now he has to die…"

Addison spoke slowly, carefully choosing her words. "William stole my dignity. He used me, and when I didn't want him, when I didn't love him in return because I knew he was a sick man devoid of any real emotion, he took what he could get. He cheated me out of thousands of dollars, and then when I complained, it cost me my job, and I learned that within a month or so my children and I were going to find ourselves out on the street… that's when I decided to take matters into my own hands and blackmail him. I intended to show him what it feels like to have your world come crashing down around you—to be left with nothing. Trust me. The death you have planned for me here means nothing in comparison to what that's like. No amount of suffering can top what he's done to me. Or what he forced me to do in return. You can't begin to understand the humiliation I felt.

But you know, I will repay him, even in death, if that's what it takes."

Hammons sat for a long time in silence, finishing off the whiskey. When the bottle was empty, he turned and climbed the stairs without bothering to lock the cage. Addison knew it was a win, but only a small one. Eventually, he would have to figure out what to do with her. And she wasn't placing any bets on him letting her walk out of there alive.

WILLIAM WOKE to the sound of his phone buzzing. He must have drifted off and had been dreaming of Addison. They were back in Capri. He was standing on the beach, and she was in the water, when all of a sudden she began drifting further and further away from shore. She was calling to him for help, but his feet wouldn't budge. He was stuck in the sand and slowly it was changing to quicksand. He was sinking further and further, and there was nothing he could do to stop it. He couldn't reach her and he knew it. They were both going down.

Taking his phone, he went to the sink and splashed cold water on his face. He quickly dried his eyes and checked his phone. Two new texts. William gasped as he opened the first one. It was a picture of Addison: naked, bloodied, bruised, and beaten. He felt tears sting his eyes. Running, he barged into the room his security team had set up in. Out of breath, he panted. "Anything?"

All eyes were on him.

Carl stood and ushered William to a chair. "Sit," he ordered. "What is it, William? You're as pale as a ghost."

William exhaled and handed his phone to Carl. "It's me. This is my fault."

Carl took his phone and examined the contents: two

texts, two incredibly graphic photos of Addison Greyer naked and badly beaten, and a demand:

William, we play by my rules now. If you ever want to see the woman you love again, meet me where Middle Creek Road and Monarch Ranch Road intersect, tomorrow at noon, sharp. Come alone and unarmed. Do not notify the authorities. Do not bring members of your security team. There will be a car waiting there with keys in it and a phone. Get in, drive, and wait for my call. Do exactly as I say. If you break any of my rules, she dies. If you fail my test, the next text you receive will be a video of Addison Greyer's beheading.

Carl handed the phone to one of the security guys. "See if you can pull any data from that. I think the intersection he mentions isn't too far from where Mrs. Greyer's vehicle was found. Get me the maps. And run all of the home sites within a hundred-mile radius. It's remote. We need to find out who lives there."

Carl ushered William to the living room. He sat with his head in his hands. "She's the only thing I've ever really loved. Goddammit, Carl, *I did this*. Whoever this is, is doing it because of me," he said with a heavy sigh. "If she's harmed any further than she already has been, I don't know what I'll do."

Carl nodded. "I understand. And it's my opinion that we hand this over to the FBI and let them do what they do. This is serious, William. The photographs clearly show us what this perpetrator is capable of. I don't think we should play around here."

William stood and walked to the window, taking in the skyline. But the only thing William could think about was the fact that Addison was out there somewhere, hurt and in danger. It was his fault. He never should've gotten involved, knowing it was putting her at risk. Not to mention, he'd known that he hadn't properly protected her. He should have known better, he was a target and because she was seeing him, she would be, too. But out of all the questions that plagued him, weighing so heavily on his mind, there was one that bothered him the most. Why hadn't he fought harder? *He could've won. He always won.*

As it stood, it was quite possible that Addison would die at the hands of this madman. Not only would it be his fault but also, she would never know how much he truly loved her because he was a coward. When the going got tough, he ran, and yet here he was.

William cleared his throat. "No, Carl. We're doing as he says— no cops. I'll use every dime I have to my name, if I have to, to nail this bastard. But no cops," he said, shaking his head. "First, we'll play by his rules. And then we'll play by mine."

ADDISON STRUGGLED AGAINST THE CHAINS. She scooted inch-by- inch, careful not to make too much noise. It must have taken hours, but finally she reached the edge of the cage. Unfortunately for her, that was about the time there was no more give in the chains. She was stuck.

Searching high and low for a way out, she was desperate to come up with a solution. There was no way to get the cuffs off of her wrists. Her ankles had a little more give. But not much. There was nothing more she could do. She'd have to buy time and earn Scott Hammons' trust. The only problem was Addison didn't have time. She was losing ground. She'd seen enough movies to know that the longer she was held captive the less likely she was to get out alive.

Suddenly, it dawned on her. What if she were being watched? Scott would see that she had stretched her chains, trying to escape. Fear overtook her and she began shaking badly. She scooted inch-by-inch back to the center of the cage, each inch excruciatingly painful as her wounds brushed against the cold hard concrete. She sobbed, defeated, as she thought of her boys and the last time she saw their faces, laughing on the kitchen floor as she tickled them silly. *They had to know by now that something was wrong.* She imagined them crying, worried about her, alone, their mother and father both gone. Surely, Patrick would come home once he'd heard. *God, she hoped someone was searching for her. They had to be.*

Once back in her rightful spot in the middle of the cage, she lay there, the last few weeks replaying in her mind. So much had happened. She thought of William and the time they'd spent together. She wondered why it had taken so long for her to admit that she had feelings for him. Partly, it was because she was married and had a family, but there was something more, too. She had been scared—scared of getting hurt. Scared of putting it all on the line. It wasn't until she found herself in this situation—naked, shackled, bleeding, and lying to save both their lives—that she realized what pain really meant. She would've gotten hurt either way. She should have just admitted that she loved him and spent their final days together, happy and oblivious. Now, she was in a race against time, realizing that William loved her enough to fall into Scott Hammons' trap. She knew that he would come for her, and that it would be her fault when he was murdered. Worst of all, he would die, thinking what they had hadn't mattered to her. She knew she couldn't let that happen.

Then and there, Addison devised a plan to break free, realizing that if she didn't die at the hands of Scott Hammons, she'd die of dehydration, starvation, or infection. Her time was up.

~

ADDISON LAY AS STILL as she could, waiting for the footsteps on the stairs. When they came, she inhaled once more, knowing what she had to do. Slowly, Scott Hammons descended. She heard him stop, likely glancing her way. She could smell the whiskey on him even from across the room. He walked over to the table, picking up his tools of the trade: Tools of domination. Tools that made him superior. He wasn't looking to become allies. He planned to beat her into submission. As a Dominatrix who had studied psychology and human behavior, she understood his techniques all too well.

"You're sleeping again," he called out. "What did I tell you about sleeping?"

Addison exhaled quietly but ignored his question. He asked again, demanding that she wake up. She could tell by the way he slurred his words that he was drunk. She said a silent prayer this would give her a slight advantage.

Scott walked to the cage. He paused, noticing it wasn't locked. She could feel his presence, she could feel him standing there, thinking. She heard the whip rise and fall and felt it slash her skin. Still, she didn't budge.

"Goddammit," he huffed. Addison felt him kneel beside her. She could tell he was watching her to see if she was breathing. She held her breath, trying her best to appear dead. But there was one problem. She didn't hear the keys rattling. If he didn't have the keys, she didn't have a chance.

"Motherfucker," he spat.

Addison could feel herself growing faint. She was close to passing out. Maybe close to death, she wasn't sure. She was just about to concede to taking a breath when finally she heard him stand and leave the cage. She gasped quietly, but only once, hopeful his back was turned. A small amount of air filled her lungs. But it wasn't enough. She gasped again, forcing more air in just as she heard him coming toward her along with the beautiful sound of keys clanging together.

Scott Hammons kneeled down beside her and pressed his fingers to her wrist in search of a pulse. Addison realized she had mere seconds. She sprung up, reached for his eyeballs, and clawed, digging as hard as she could. He let out a scream as she wrapped the chain around his neck. She twisted, squeezing as hard as she could until she heard the keys hit the floor with a thud. Scott struggled against the chains, fighting back, until Addison was almost sure he'd break free. She pulled harder, watching his face turn blue. Finally, when he stopped struggling, she let go and frantically grabbed the set of keys lying at his feet. Shaking heavily, she unlocked her ankles first and then freed her wrists. Once free, she bolted for the door.

Once she'd reached the top of the stairs, she paused. *Shit.* The door was locked. She didn't remember hearing him lock the door. Addison glanced backward over her shoulder, and then hurriedly tried each of the keys one by one until finally the third key she tried fit. She twisted and the door gave way.

The light hit her and it was almost too much. She squinted and scanned the old rickety farmhouse in search of a door. Once she spotted it, she bolted, noticing it was dark outside. Naked, she realized there wasn't time to remedy the situation. She had to get out. Now. As she gripped the handle, she heard a familiar voice call from behind. "Open it and you're dead."

Addison turned to see Scott aiming a gun at her. Turning the handle, she heard the first shot fire off, right before it grazed her shoulder. Addison fled as she heard several more shots ring out behind her. She ran as fast as her bare feet would take her, making sure to zigzag the way she'd once seen on TV, adrenaline coursing through her veins. It was pitch black out, making it impossible to see anything in front of her. Eventually, she heard the shots stop. But she didn't stop running. Before long the sound of gunfire was replaced by footsteps closing in behind her. She made a hard right and ran and ran until she felt water beneath her feet. She could make out what appeared to be bushes up ahead, and unable to go any further, unable to breathe, she decided to hide. She army crawled her way in, burrowing herself, trying to become invisible as the branches pierced her skin.

She waited, she knew he'd find her, it was just a matter of time. In the meantime, she listened as he called out for her. He screamed profanities, telling her she was going to die. Addison could tell that he was close, that he was closing in. She just couldn't gauge how close. She held her breath and counted. She'd only gotten to twenty-three when she felt the fire ants begin to bite. Her skin stung but she held her breath, trying to remain as quiet as possible. Eventually, the tears came; hot tears spilled onto her cheeks, and by the time they'd run out, the pain began to subside. She felt numb. Addison listened for Scott's footsteps. It sounded as though they were growing further away. She couldn't be sure though, so she stayed put. At some point, she'd have to crawl out and keep running. Addison knew it was just a matter of time before the sun came up. He'd find her then. At the same time she was paralyzed by fear, knowing he was out there waiting. Scott Hammons hadn't retreated, he wasn't far away. He was watching and waiting; she could feel it.

WILLIAM WENT against what everyone had told him to do and got in the car parked at the intersection of Monarch and Middle Creek Roads, just like he was ordered to do. In the middle of nowhere, he drove until he heard the phone ring.

He answered and waited for further instructions. "Turn right onto Mayfield in half a mile. Park a quarter of a mile down on the right hand side."

William felt the sweat drip from his brow as he made the turn. He knew his team would be close behind, that they were tracking his every move via a device they'd planted in his shoe. He only had to keep his shoes on his feet and stay alive long enough to close the ten-minute gap. He did as he was instructed and pulled onto Mayfield Road. He glanced at his surroundings. There was nothing but trees. He prayed that he was close to Addison, that she was still alive, and that she could somehow feel he was going to find her. William suddenly felt sick to his stomach. Pulling off after a quarter mile down, he stopped and opened the car door. He leaned out and hurled onto the gravel road. After a few minutes, he watched a silver car come into view up ahead. The car slowed, pulling over. In the driver's seat sat his old friend, Scott Hammons.

Well, I'll be damned was the last thought William remembered before the stun gun pierced his skin. As he lay there, face down in the gravel, he was grateful, certain he could hear the familiar sound of a helicopter closing in overhead.

WILLIAM'S SECURITY team was on the scene within a matter of minutes and as he turned onto Mayfield Road, they made sure to stay far enough behind so as not to be seen. But they were able to close in just as Scott Hammons was attempting but failing to load William into the trunk of his car. The FBI arrived on scene moments after Carl planted Hammons' face into the pavement. "Where is she, Scott?" he demanded. When there was no answer, Carl landed a crushing blow to Scott's right temple.

An hour later, the FBI raided the old farmhouse only to find Addison wasn't there. "I'm sorry," Carl explained to William. "They haven't located her."

William ran his fingers through his hair. He'd refused medical treatment and was supposed to be recovering in a makeshift trailer that had been set up by the FBI. "They're searching the place now," Carl added. "They're pretty confident that's where he's been holding her."

William jumped up. "Where is the bastard?" he demanded. "Let me interrogate him."

"They're doing everything they can to get answers, William." Carl said, placing his hand on William's shoulder.

"How far is the house?"

"About two miles."

William stood. "Good. Then let's go."

Carl sighed and stepped in front of the trailer door. "I'm afraid we can't. The Feds have the place sealed off. It's a crime scene, William."

He sat back down and placed his head in his hands, his shoulders shaking as he began to sob. It was something that he hadn't done in a very long time—not since he was a little boy, the last time he'd found his life at the mercy of a madman.

PATRICK GREYER WAS HOLDING his boys, anxiously waiting on word on his missing wife. It all seemed so surreal. *How could this be happening? If anything happened to her, he didn't know what he would do.*

Luckily for Patrick, he hadn't received the papers his wife had sent asking that the two be legally separated. If he had, he would've started asking questions a lot sooner. Questions like why in the world William Hartman seemed so interested in his wife's case or why he was throwing reward money towards the investigation. These were questions that would come eventually, in time, but for now, Patrick was consumed with getting his wife home safely. He swore to God that if she returned home alive he would see to it that nothing, neither jobs nor people, would ever separate the two of them again.

CHAPTER TWENTY

Addison Greyer heard the helicopters circling overhead, and still she wouldn't, couldn't make herself come out. It wasn't safe, not yet. She had to stay put. Dehydrated, weak, and eaten by fire ants, she wasn't sure how long she could wait it out. She drifted off and found herself dreaming of the boys playing in the backyard as Max chased them while barking. It wasn't until much later that Addison would realize that it was likely the search dogs that found her that had been barking. By the time she was located, she was near death and hypothermic. It was the heat imaging sensors on the helicopter that circled overhead that ultimately saved her life. Search and rescue dogs were then sent in, and they, along with a team of FBI agents, found her unconscious in the bushes.

Doctors later explained that she was lucky she was found when she was, that she had been within hours of death. When Addison woke in the ICU, William was standing over her. Opening just one eye, she peeked at him and mustered a smile. He looked almost unrecognizable, a different version of the William she knew, older with worry lines.

William stroked her face. "Hey there."

She tried to speak, but her mouth was too dry to get anything out.

"Shhh," he whispered, brushing her hair away from her face. "Don't talk. Just rest, ok? Let me do all of the talking."

She was too weak to do anything else and so she simply nodded.

"Listen—" he told her, speaking in a hurried tone. "I only have a minute. Your husband is on his way up. But I need to tell you I'm going to be back— later today, tomorrow, and every day after that. I love you, Addison. I love you more than anything. And I'm so sorry. I'm so sorry for so many things, but most of all for not fighting for you. I promise . . . I *swear* to you it won't ever happen again."

Addison had wanted to tell him that it was okay, but she was drowsy. She dozed off, and when she woke again, she wondered if she'd dreamt it all, if William had ever really been there at all. She glanced around the room until her eyes landed on Patrick. "Hi," he said, his face lighting up. "I've been waiting for hours. They said not to wake you."

Addison tried to speak, but only managed to get two words out. "The boys?"

Patrick smiled. "They're fine. They know doctors are checking you out. They know you're sick but that you're ok and will be home soon. The doctors said that once we get you moved out of the ICU, they'll be allowed to come visit," he told her, proudly. "Of course, we need to get you looking better first."

She nodded, satisfied, she let herself drift off to the place where she dreamed of William.

Later when she woke, he was there with her, almost as if he'd manifested from her dream.

Sensing her confusion, he spoke. "Hey beautiful. It's late... or early depending on how you look at it. Patrick went home to be with the kids. Sondra tells me they're doing great in spite of everything. Just anxious to come see you. I tried to pull some strings to get them in here. Nothing has panned out yet. They tell me rules are rules," he told her shaking his head. "But I'm not giving up."

Addison licked her lips, although it did nothing for her. Her mouth, everything felt so dry. William leaned down, and kissed her forehead. "Water," she asked.

He nodded. Holding a straw up to her lips, William ordered her to drink. "I told them this is for me. I knew you'd need it," he smiled. "It's our secret, ok?"

After draining the Styrofoam cup, unable to stop herself she drifted off again.

Next time when she awoke, it was Patrick and Penny that were standing over her. They whispered in hushed tones, and it took Addison a moment to make out what they were saying. She pretended to be asleep, not ready to face them both. When it didn't stop, the gossip, that is, she opened her eyes and prepared herself for what was about to come.

It was Penny who spoke first. "We're so disappointed in you, Addison. Good God," she sighed, exasperated. "What could've possibly gotten into that head of yours?"

Addison didn't speak.

Patrick followed up. "We know the truth, Addison. Just tell me what were you thinking?" he asked, nodding in her direction. "Look at the shape you're in. Look where you've landed yourself."

She looked away. Penny continued. "We know about your relationship with William Hartman. I must say I warned my son. I knew that you were up to something, but *this* . . . well, this is beyond disappointing—beyond what I could have imagined. You've hurt your husband and your children. I just don't get it," she said throwing up her hands. "How could you?"

All at once, Addison found her voice. "This doesn't concern you. In fact, nothing I do concerns you. You don't know what you're talking about and I'd like you to leave."

Penny scoffed. "I'm not going anywhere. Not until you give my son the decency of some answers."

Addison pressed the call button and glared at her mother in law. "You aren't on the visitors list."

She looked at her son, her mouth agape. "I didn't realize there was such a thing."

"Well, there is now," Addison said.

Patrick interrupted. "The FBI is waiting to interview you. They asked us not to speak of it until you're well enough for them to get in here, but I will say this: Mr. Hammons defense is that you were his Dominatrix. He considers what happened a session gone badly. He's told the Feds that you were on drugs and sleeping with William Hartman," Patrick told her looking away. He turned toward his mother and then back toward Addison as though he were choosing his words carefully. "Now, ordinarily I'd assume that this was all false, simply accusations made up by a crazy person, but then William Hartman went and hired a legal team to represent you should this thing go to trial," he added, running his hands through his hair. "So, I gotta ask Addison, what is going on?"

Addison shook her head. "This isn't the time. But, given that you guys seem to have it already figured out, I think it'd be best if you both leave. I'm tired."

Penny chimed in. "Here's the thing, Addison. You're irresponsible, and quite frankly, pathetic actions are going to tarnish my family's name. Your husband and children are going to be the laughing stock of this town. Now, clearly you've made your bed, and, by the looks of things, you're lying in it. But my husband and I are well prepared to save our son and our grandchildren. Make no mistake," she promised. "We intend to do just that."

She pushed the call button for a nurse once again only to have Penny wave her away. "Don't bother," she told her. "I was just leaving. Patrick," she added, "I'll see you back at the house."

Addison nodded at her husband and then toward the door. "No, you should go, too."

He hesitated. "Mother, wait for me outside, would you?"

Patrick turned to Addison. She refused to look at him. "Don't do this, Addison. Don't shut me out. We can fix this. Whatever you've done—we can turn it around. Let your rich little lover boy pay for a defense," he shrugged. "I don't care. But you and I, we have to work this out. If not for us, then for the boys. Think of them for a moment, would you."

Addison looked him straight in the eye. "I am thinking of the kids. But I'm sorry, Patrick, you made your choice months ago when you checked out—actually, come to think of it, maybe even years ago. Other than logistics, I don't see that there is anything left to work out."

His jaw tightened. "I'm warning you," he said. "Don't do this. I'll take the boys. I'll fight for custody. I'll take everything. And from where I'm standing, it doesn't appear that you have much of a leg to stand on."

Feeling the blow she knew was coming, Addison did her best to keep a straight face. "You should go now, Patrick. Your mother is waiting. We can discuss this later."

He smiled then. "That's the girl I love," he murmured, before patting her head. "I knew, with a little explanation, you'd begin to see things my way."

She flinched when he bent down to kiss her cheek. She shifted and then watched him walk to the door. He stopped, turning just inside the doorframe. He looked back at her and smiled. "Oh, and tell that bastard William Hartman that if he comes around here again, I'll personally see to it that our kids are in China by Sunday."

And there it was: the final blow. Addison had dozens of battery marks, scratches, and even sutures, but the physical wounds she suffered paled in comparison to this. This one was the blow that would most certainly do her in.

∼

PATRICK GREYER HAD UNDERESTIMATED his wife. Never in a million years could he have imagined that his Addison had it in her to beat up on rich men and earn a living while doing it. He also never imagined that a guy as wealthy and powerful as William Hartman would fall in love with her and attempt to steal her from him right under his very nose. But somehow that was exactly what happened, which left Patrick to sort through the mess.

For one thing, he wasn't letting her go. He had worked long and hard at their marriage and wasn't giving up what was rightfully and legally his, not for money, not for anything. Speaking of money, he needed to find it. In addition to all of the other secrets she'd been keeping, Patrick had also learned his wife had been earning a pretty penny for what she was doing behind his back, but what he hadn't accounted for was how adept she could be at hiding that money.

He saw the look in his wife's eyes when he confronted her. She knew that he knew. He had expected her to lie. He'd hoped that she'd continue trying to deceive him. But when she didn't, it told him everything that he needed to know—she was no longer in love with him. It didn't matter though. He'd be damned if he'd give up that easily. He'd be damned if he let her just up and take off with his children. Patrick wasn't the losing kind, he'd make her see that. There was, of course, a bit of ego involved in his decision, he knew there was no way that he could ever compete with William Hartman and come out on top, so Patrick did the only thing he knew to do to save his marriage and keep from losing his family: he used his children as pawns. Sure, perhaps his wife wasn't in love with him right now, but he would change that. He'd make her see that it was possible to have again what they'd once had. He certainly wasn't going to stand by and let her choose another man with the whole world watching. He'd seen the news. The story was everywhere. He only had to come out on top.

He just had to keep his mistress out of the way if he had any chance at all. Patrick understood he was running on borrowed time, that once Michele realized he never intended on coming back she would be quick to let the cat out of the bag. She would only buy his lies for so long. Even still, he had his plan, and he wouldn't allow her or anyone else to stop him from seeing it through.

SONDRA SHEEHAN WAS ABSOLUTELY GLOWING the day that Addison woke up and found her sitting next to her hospital bed. She was finally starting to show, and although she hadn't quite forgiven Sondra, Addison had never seen her more radiant.

As Sondra stood, Addison placed her hand on Sondra's belly, and for a moment, time stood still.

Finally, Sondra spoke. "It's a boy," she whispered, her eyes lighting up as she spoke. "What in the world am I going to do with a little boy?"

Addison smiled weakly "You're going to love him with everything you have."

Sondra placed her hand on Addison's. "You know . . . I

never wanted this, but somehow I think it was meant to be this way. Already, I love him more than I ever thought possible… I mean, I've never been more worried about anything in my whole life."

Addison shifted in the bed, wincing in pain as she attempted to sit up. "Welcome to motherhood."

"Addison," Sondra said, her expression full of concern. "I'm incredibly sorry for putting you in this position. I know there's a lot to discuss… and I know how angry you must be…"

"I don't know what to say…"

"Well, I hope you'll say that once you're fully recovered that you'll come back to the staffing agency. Because of what happened, we've made huge changes to policy. Also, I know this may not be the time, but we'd like to offer you a settlement of sorts."

Addison studied Sondra's face. "You're nothing if not a businesswoman, huh? And just when I was beginning to like you, too."

"It's a decent settlement, Addison. You're entitled to it," Sondra's voice broke as she continued. "But that's not why I'm here. I just wanted you to know, in case you were lying here worried. Actually, I came to ask you a favor…"

Addison cocked her head slightly.

"It's about William. Obviously, he knows everything, and in turn he's not speaking to me. I understand why, but I want to ask you if you'll promise me something?"

Addison waited.

Sondra took a deep breath. "Promise me that you'll keep an eye on him—that you'll let him love you and that you'll love him back. I know it's complicated, Addison, but promise me you'll try."

She stared at the floor, unable to meet Sondra's eye. "I can't promise you that…"

"Seriously, Addison, look around," Sondra told her, her voice dropping. "Can't you see he is in love with you? He fills your room with flowers, hires an armed guard to sit outside your door 24/7, provides you with the best legal team there is, and is currently sleeping in a room down the hall just so he never has to leave your side. All the while, he waits with the most pained expression I've ever seen, by the way, for your husband to come and go."

Addison's breath caught. She eyed the orchids that filled her room. "I know."

"Then what exactly is the problem?"

Addison locked eyes with Sondra. "I can't promise anything right now. Just trust that, eventually, I'll make things right. But for now, I really can't offer any more than that. I know how it sounds. But it's complicated... so you'll just have to take my word for it..."

Sondra patted Addison's leg and let it be. "Talk to him for me, ok? Put in a good word, will ya?"

"Absolutely," Addison replied, surprised that Sondra didn't pry. She smiled, grateful for small victories. William might buy her lies, but Sondra never would.

ADDISON STROKED William's hair as she stared at his head lying in her lap. She memorized every detail, knowing what was coming. She was about to break his heart.

William looked up at her suddenly, as though he sensed something was wrong. He searched her face as she took him in, allowing his deep blue eyes to burn into her memory. As long as she lived, she would never forget that moment, the way that he looked at her.

"I hear you're going home tomorrow," he said, raising his brow. "What am I going to do when I can't just sneak down the hall and see your face? I was thinking about all of the ways I would miss you, and I was wondering . . . I was thinking that maybe you should come home with me."

"Come home with you?" She wasn't sure what she'd been expecting, but it wasn't that.

He nodded. "That way I can kiss you whenever I want to. I could get a place where you could rest, where the boys could run and play, where I could protect you. We could be happy, Addison."

She took a deep breath, her eyes never leaving his. "I love you, William. I need you to know that. Tell me that you know that."

He grinned, flashing the smile she adored so much. "I know that."

Addison took a strand of his hair and wrapped it around her little finger. "I can't come home with you," she said, blurting it out. "But it's worse than that. . . . we can't be together right now."

"Why not?"

Addison exhaled. "I need to focus on my marriage right now. It's complicated. Let's just leave it at that."

William stood, yanking his head from her grasp. "Are you fucking kidding me? He doesn't give a shit about you, Addison."

She swallowed. "No, I'm not kidding you."

"I let you go once. I don't intend on doing it again."

Addison sat up, trying to close the distance she was creating. "I just need some time, ok. That's all. I need you to trust me."

William paused, rubbing his chin. Addison knew this was what he did when he was thinking, questioning himself. "He's having an affair, Addison."

"I know."

William turned on his heel and glared at her, confused. "What do you mean, *you know*? Seriously? Goddamn, Addison, I never had you pegged as one who would put up with that shit."

"Just what I said—I know. I received an anonymous envelope weeks ago. I guess I should be asking you why you knew and kept it from me."

Carl. William hesitated. "I didn't want to be the reason you left him. I mean . . . I did, but I wanted it to be the *right* reason. Not the runner up. Guess not much has changed though, has it?"

She considered telling him the truth, that Patrick was blackmailing her, threatening to take the kids, but changed directions instead, knowing that if William knew the truth he'd put up a fight. He'd insist that she put up a fight and going to war wasn't in her children's best interest. Not with what she had going on hanging over her head. It was quite possible that she could lose and that was a risk she wasn't willing to take. She took a deep breath in. "Once Scott Hammons' case goes to trial, everything is going to come out. I'm going to be painted as a philandering whore, every mistake I've ever made exposed for the entire world to see. I can't let this destroy my family, William. If I leave now, our lives will be irrevocably altered. I need to ride this out," she said, chewing at her bottom lip. "I need time, William."

"Fuck time. What's going to come out will come out. Which reminds me . . . You and I have a lot to discuss. I've hired the best legal team money can buy. They know what they're dealing with, and they're perfectly capable of handling this. This is bullshit, Addison, it's an excuse, and we both know it."

Addison tried a different method. "They're freeing Scott on bond, William. If you and I are together, who knows what . . ."

William sighed, sitting on the edge of her bed. "How much time are you asking for?"

"Just until the trial's over."

"And what then?"

"Then I'll leave."

William curled up in the bed next to Addison and kissed her face. "But that could be months away."

"I know," she said, looking away. "But I need you to trust me on this. Please. It's not that long. If you love me, William, you'll either wait or you'll let me go. It's your choice, but I want you to at least consider my point of view. I have children to think about. I have to protect them. They are, and always will be, my number one priority," she told him, meeting his eye. "If we're going to be together, you have to understand that and be willing to accept it."

"Ok," he said, running his hands through his hair. "What is it that you're asking exactly?"

She swallowed. "I'm asking that we cease contact until the trial is complete. In light of all that is about to come out about us— and about Seven— and my role there, it's just too risky."

William intertwined his fingers with hers. "I'm just not sure I can do it."

Addison squeezed his hand. "I'm not sure you have any other choice."

ADDISON AND WILLIAM said their tearful goodbyes early the next morning, standing in her hospital room, each of them promising the other that they'd be together again once the trial was over and Scott Hammons had been convicted of kidnapping and attempted murder. No matter what happened in between, they agreed.

As the weeks went by, life slowly returned to a new normal. At first, William had consumed her mind nearly every waking moment. Eventually though, as the weeks gave way to months and although the pain never quite subsided, she found she was finally able to get through the day without crying.

Thanksgiving came and went as Addison immersed herself in her children. Patrick returned to the office after a few weeks, although he mostly chose to work at home. Over time, the two of them began speaking, not much, but a little here and there, as Addison tried to put on a happy front for the children.

In keeping with the facade, she'd agreed to accompany Patrick and the boys to pick out their Christmas tree. It was tradition, after all. And no matter what, they'd always be parents, so she figured it wouldn't hurt to play nice.

Maybe it was the spirit of the season, or the fact that Addison knew that it was likely their final Christmas together, but when Connor pulled the two of them together and Patrick reached for her hand, intertwining their fingers, she didn't pull away. Seeing her children happy reminded her to be happy. She owed them that much.

Lost in thought, it was Patrick who brought her back to reality. "Look, boys," he called out. "It's Mommy's friend, Mr. Hartman." Patrick added, gripping Addison's hand tighter as she tried to pull away.

Just up ahead, she noticed William, the two of them locking eyes for a brief second before his gaze fell to her hand still inside of Patrick's. Addison could see the pain twisted on William's face as he registered what he was seeing. Still, he closed the gap between them.

Patrick extended his hand and William hesitantly shook it, not taking his eyes off of Addison. "William, what a pleasure it is running into you here. I'm sure you remember my wife, Addison. But I don't think you've met these guys...these are our children: Connor, Parker and James."

William smiled at the boys, shaking their hands one by one. "Well, I'd better be going," he said, at once. Glaring at Addison, he added. "It's so nice to have finally met you guys."

Addison watched, speechless, as everything around her happened in slow motion.

"Once this trial business is said and done, my wife and I and these little guys you see here are heading back to China. I think we're all looking forward to getting away."

Addison's mouth gaped as Patrick spoke. "I don't think . . ."

William put his hands up to stop her, his expression unreadable. "Like I said, I've got to run. Merry Christmas."

And just like that, William turned on his heel and walked in the other direction. Addison watched him until he was just a tiny speck blended in among the crowd. But just as she thought she'd lost sight of him, William turned, their eyes locking for the briefest of seconds, until she felt her hand being tugged in the opposite direction. Her eyes welled up; the tears spilled over as it took every ounce of willpower she had in her not to turn and run to him. Although, she couldn't say for sure, she swore she saw the slightest hint of a smile form upon his lips. Wiping her eyes, she searched the crowd again. But just as fast as William had appeared, he was gone.

A NOTE FROM BRITNEY

Dear Reader,

I hope you enjoyed reading *Bedrock*. If you have a moment and you'd like to let me know what you thought, feel free to drop me an email. I enjoy hearing from readers.

Writing a book is an interesting adventure, it's a bit like inviting people into your brain to rummage around. *Look where my imagination took me. These are the kinds stories I like...*

That feeling is often intense and unforgettable. And mostly, a ton of fun.

With that in mind—thank you again for reading my work. I don't have the backing or the advertising dollars of big publishing, but hopefully I have something better... readers who like the same kind of stories I do. If you are one of them, please share with your friends and consider helping out by doing one (or all) of these quick things:

1. Visit my Review Page and write a 30 second review (even short ones make a big difference).

(http://britneyking.com/aint-too-proud-to-beg-for-reviews/)

Many readers don't realize what a difference reviews make but they make ALL the difference.

2. Drop me an email and let me know you left a review. This way I can enter you into my monthly drawing for signed paperback copies.

(britney@britneyking.com)

3. Point your psychological thriller loving friends to their <u>free copies</u> of my work. My favorite friends are those who introduce me to books I might like. **(http://www.britneyking.com)**

4. If you'd like to make sure you don't miss anything, to receive an email whenever I release a new title, sign up for my New Release Newsletter.

(https://britneyking.com/new-release-alerts/)

Thanks for helping, and for reading my work. It means a lot.

Britney King

Austin, Texas

January 2018

Britney King lives in Austin, Texas with her husband, children, two dogs, one ridiculous cat, and a partridge in a peach tree.

When she's not wrangling the things mentioned above, she writes psychological, domestic and romantic thrillers set in suburbia.

Without a doubt, she thinks connecting with readers is the best part of this gig. You can find Britney online here:

Email: britney@britneyking.com
Web: https://britneyking.com
Facebook: https://www.facebook.com/BritneyKingAuthor
Instagram: https://www.instagram.com/britneyking_/
Twitter: https://twitter.com/BritneyKing_
Goodreads: https://bit.ly/BritneyKingGoodreads
Pinterest: https://www.pinterest.com/britneyking_/

Happy reading.

ACKNOWLEDGMENTS

I would especially like to thank my husband and children for supporting my dream to write (and complete—I have to add that) this novel. For not complaining (too much) about the messy house or the times my eyes glazed over when you were talking to me because I was "thinking about my book, again." But most of all, for your continued tolerance with each new endeavor I choose to pursue. One of them is going to pay off. I just know it. :)

Last, but certainly not least; I would like to thank each and every one of you for taking the time to read my work. It means a lot.

Around The Bend

Around The Bend, is a heart-pounding standalone which traces the journey of a well-to-do suburban housewife, and her life as it unravels, thanks to the secrets she keeps. If she were the only one with things she wanted to keep hidden, then maybe it wouldn't have turned out so bad. But she wasn't.

Somewhere With You / Book One

Anywhere With You / Book Two

The With You Series Box Set

The With You Series at its core is a deep love story about unlikely friends who travel the world; trying to find themselves, together and apart. Packed with drama and adventure along with a heavy dose of suspense, it has been compared to The Secret Life of Walter Mitty and Love, Rosie.

"Totally on the edge of my seat the whole time I was reading it, couldn't put it down!" – Book Addict Mumma

"As a sequel this book works extremely well, as a stand alone thriller it is also very good but clearly readers would be left a little lost about the back story (in which case read 'Bedrock' first)." —Paul Little, Little Ebook Reviews

"I haven't felt this many emotions in a book in a very long time." – Saints and Sinners Books

"The writing... goodness... I would have never thought this was the author's first foray into Adult Romance. The writing... Again... Wonderful!! — Gretchen Anderson, Battery Operated Book Blog

As a married mother of three, Addison Greyer has always been known for doing the right thing. Hoping to keep it that way, she's fought like hell to avoid falling for the mysterious, highly successful, albeit broken man whom the world knows as William Hartman.

But there's just something about that which is forbidden...

From the way he looks at her to the way he so eloquently professes his love via written letters--there's something undeniable in the way he makes her feel.

With the two of them separated by a trial, public opinion, and a marriage that seems to be unraveling by the hour, the pressure mounts, and Addison soon realizes the price she'll pay to keep everyone else happy.

Until it becomes pretty clear that some rules were made to be broken.

In this highly anticipated sequel to Bedrock, Addison learns that you can't help who you fall in love with--and it almost never happens the way you think it should.

BREAKING BEDROCK

BRITNEY KING

COPYRIGHT

BREAKING BEDROCK is a work of fiction. Names, characters, places, images, and incidents are products of the author's imagination or are used fictitiously and are not to be construed as real. Any resemblance to actual events, locales, organizations, persons, living or dead, is entirely coincidental and not intended by the author. The scanning, uploading, and distribution of this book without permission is a theft of the author's intellectual property. No part of this publication may be used, shared or reproduced in any manner whatsoever without written permission except in the case of brief quotations embodied in critical articles and reviews. If you would like permission to use material from the book (other than for review purposes), please contact https://britneyking.com/contact/

Thank you for your support of the author's rights.

Hot Banana Press
Front Cover Design by Lisa Wilson
Back Cover Design by Britney King
Cover Image by Sebastian Kullas
Copy Editing by TW Manuscript Services
Proofread by Proofreading by the Page

Copyright © 2013 by Britney King LLC. All Rights Reserved.

First Edition: 2013
ISBN: 978-0-9892184-7-4 (Paperback)
ISBN: 978-0-9892184-2-9 (All E-Books)
britneyking.com

For the William in my life,
we should all be so lucky . . .

CHAPTER ONE

This is a story about truth, to be sure. Who's truth, well, that's for you to decide. More than that, it's about good versus evil; it's about winning and losing. It's about the darkness that lives inside each of us. However, strip it all down and you'll find underneath, it's a love story. But then, really, aren't they all?

It is my belief that love is mostly about showing up. It's about showing up in the good times and especially in the bad. It's about being there, and continuing to be there, particularly when the going gets tough. Because that's the thing about love, isn't it? The going *always* gets tough. But, if you can manage to dig your heels in, day in and day out, no matter what life brings, I think you'll find that you might just come out on top. In time, you might come to find that while love and what you thought you knew of it, may in fact, look very different than you'd imagined, it's there nonetheless. Even when it's dark and unpredictable. I find, all the best things are.

～

Addison Greyer pulled the sweatshirt over her head, stuffed her keys and phone in the pocket, grabbed her pepper spray and headed out for the run she so desperately needed. It was a cold, dreary morning, the kind where the cold settles in your bones until it hurts. Gripping the pepper spray tightly, she rounded her driveway, taking off in full sprint, pushing herself harder and faster than she had in some time. Although her eyes stung and her lungs burned, Addison knew better than to give in. She knew better than to stop. Not today. Today there was no stopping. Today was about pushing through the pain, today was about getting to the other side, only to find there is no other side. It didn't matter. Today she would run and run and run until she couldn't.

She would run and she would let her mind drift back and forth over the past few months as though searching for a clue, any tiny shred of evidence that may have simply been overlooked. She'd played out this scenario hundreds of times, hoping that she could find something she'd overlooked, a missing piece that if found, would make everything clear. She needed to run. But, she also needed things to make sense.

It wasn't unusual that William Hartman weighed heavily on Addison's mind, and today was certainly no different. Unfortunately, the situation had become significantly worse over the past twenty-four hours, and no matter what she did or how she tried to keep herself busy, she couldn't stop her thoughts from returning to the letter. Her mind replayed the words over and over. She'd memorized them. They'd etched their way into her soul, just like the cold weighed on her bones, only worse. She recalled now, her breath heaving against the cold, how she'd traced her finger around the smooth edges of her finest stationery and then carefully tucked it in the envelope. She'd taken the letter out again just to run her fingers over it one last time as though maybe, just maybe, she could tuck a little bit of herself in with it. She closed her eyes and silently prayed that the letter's recipient might feel her, that forgiveness might be nestled between the lines. She even entertained the idea that if she were to concentrate hard enough, perhaps she might undo what she'd done—how quickly she'd emailed the courier and scheduled for a pick-up before calling to cancel, only to finally call back and schedule once more.

Still, no matter how her heart struggled against what she'd done, her mind knew it was the right thing to do. Addison hadn't been able to forgive herself after what would be forever dubbed "the disastrous Christmas-tree event." It had been that night as she pressed her head to the smooth cold tile of her bathroom floor, tears streaming silently down her face, that she finally understood what it was she needed to do. It was time she let him go, once and for all. She wasn't good for him. He wasn't good for her. At least not in any of the ways that mattered, when it came right down to it. That much was clear. Asking him to wait for her wasn't fair. Asking him to be something he wasn't would never work. Her life was a complete and utter mess. There wasn't room for anything else, certainly not love and all of its glorious chaos.

For starters, Scott Hammons, the man who had kidnapped and tortured her, had been arraigned, pleading not guilty, and was out on bail. He'd somehow managed to retain counsel who was able to convince a judge to allow him a pre-trial release after agreeing to a strict no-contact order, 24/7 electronic monitoring, and of course, after having posted a hefty amount of bail money. None of that mattered to Addison. No restraining order and certainly no ankle bracelet was enough to make her feel safe. She'd seen what Scott Hammons was capable of, not to mention the look in his eye at the arraignment, full of contempt. She knew he wasn't finished with her, not by a long shot. But if that weren't enough, her husband was blackmailing her to stay in a marriage that they both knew deep down, whether he wanted to admit it or not, was broken beyond repair.

Suffice it to say, not only was her life in turmoil but it was certainly no place to let love walk in. The next few months would be precarious, at least until the preliminary hearing, and quite frankly, Addison realized, there was no room for anything more than survival. Given the thoughts of Scott Hammons and what she might have to do to put an end to the situation, once and for all, Addison pushed herself harder. She embraced the cold, welcomed the pain, feeling each step as her feet pounded the payment. The faster she ran, the more the words she'd written played in her mind, words that would never, could never, be enough.

Panting hard and slightly dizzy, Addison was trying to recall whether or not she'd eaten anything that morning when a sudden movement up ahead caught her eye, causing her to stop abruptly in her tracks. After focusing in and real- izing she recognized the car, Addison sighed and braced herself, knowing exactly what was waiting for her down the road.

William Hartman turned the unassuming envelope over in his hands and considered the weight of it. No one sent letters like this anymore, and this one felt familiar, classy; impor- tant. He didn't open his own mail and whoever had sent this understood that, which meant that it could only have come from a small pool of senders. Opening it, he admired the stationery, realizing exactly who it was from and what it would say. William sank back it his chair, ran his fingers through his hair and proceeded to take it all in.

CHAPTER ONE

Dear William,

I've wanted so many times to call over the past week, but with the trial coming up, the attorneys have instructed me not to have any contact with you. In addition, it's very plausible that you have no interest in hearing from me today or any other day for that matter. But I want to tell you that I'm sorry, William. I am so very sorry for so many things. I'm sorry for making the decisions that I did, I'm sorry for dragging you into the chaos that is my life, I'm sorry that you saw what you did the other night in the park, and I will be forever sorry that I didn't have the strength in that moment to do and say all the things I should have.

There is one thing, however, that I am not sorry for: falling in love with you. I want you to know that I would give just about anything to be where you are, to be in a different time and a different place. And I want you to know, for what it's worth, that I wish I could take back the way things turned out in the park. But I can't. And the truth is, what happened has given me the clarity to understand what I need to do from here.

I need to move forward with my life, William. I need to move forward with the way things really are, the way they currently stand, not how I wish they were. I have to beat Scott Hammons in this trial. I need to prove to him, and everyone else, that what he did to me was real, that I'm *not* what or who they're going to say I am. I need to know that my children are safe and secure and I need them to know that their mother loves them and would do ANYTHING for them. For the time being, that means I need to stay in my marriage, and for what it's worth, I can't very well do that with one foot out the door. And more importantly, I cannot very well do that and at the same time be hopelessly in love with you.

I have to let go for good this time. The irony here is that it's fairly likely that you already have and that I really don't have to say any of this at all. Honestly, if we're facing facts here, it appears that we've both let go. But so long as neither of says it out loud, it can't be real, can it? I guess that's why I felt I needed to say it.

Again, I'm sorry, William. I am sorry I hurt you. I'm sorry to have been just one more person in your life to let you down. And while I regret the aftermath, I do not, for one second, regret anything that happened between us. I have been a better person for it.

I hope for you the very best that life has to offer; and I want to thank you. Thank you for loving me. But most of all, thank you for showing me a side to love I'd never known before: the best side.

A world of love,

Addison

William meticulously placed the note back in its envelope. He'd been right about one thing. It was classy; that was for sure. Suddenly needing to let off steam, he laced his running shoes and headed downstairs to the gym but not before placing a phone call that could no longer be delayed. Apparently, Addison Greyer had forgotten who she was dealing with. Too bad for her, William had just decided he was finished playing nice. This time, he wasn't fighting fair.

∼

Learn more at: britneyking.com

Made in the USA
Coppell, TX
28 August 2020

34568575R00163